SOMETHING TO THINK OF

Something to Think Of

Copyright © 2021 by P. O. Dixon

All rights reserved.

No part of this book may be reproduced in any form or by any electronic or mechanical means, including information storage and retrieval systems, without written permission from the author, except for the use of brief quotations in a book review.

This book is a work of fiction. The characters depicted in this book are fictitious or are used fictitiously. Any resemblance to actual events, locales, or persons, living or dead, is entirely coincidental.

ISBN-13: 9798536360767

DEDICATION

In memory of a dear friend

CONTENTS

Acknowledgments   vii

Chapter 1   1
A Capricious Inducement

Chapter 2   13
A Disagreeable Connection

Chapter 3   23
Very Agreeable Strangers

Chapter 4   33
A Moment's Reflection

Chapter 5   47
A Casual Acquaintance

Chapter 6   63
Exercise in Futility

Chapter 7   71
A Secret Admirer

Chapter 8   77
One Noticeable Exception

Chapter 9   91
Her Heart of Hearts

Chapter 10   99
A Way with Words

Chapter 11   109
Kindred Spirits

Chapter 12   117
A Curious Creature

Chapter 13   127
A Respectable Profession

Chapter 14   135
Cause for Concern

Chapter 15   143
In His Possession

Chapter 16 *Making Matters Worse*	149
Chapter 17 *Sinister Forces*	159
Chapter 18 *The General Understanding*	167
Chapter 19 *More Inconvenient Time*	175
Chapter 20 *Sense of Honor*	185
Chapter 21 *Her Maternal Feelings*	191
Chapter 22 *In that Manner*	197
Chapter 23 *The Happiest Woman*	203
Also by P. O. Dixon	209
About the Author	213
Connect with the Author	215

ACKNOWLEDGMENTS

Heartfelt gratitude is bestowed to Miss Jane Austen for her timeless classic, *Pride and Prejudice*, which makes all this possible.

What a joy it is imagining different paths to happily ever after for our beloved couple, Darcy and Elizabeth, and then sharing the stories with the world.

Special thanks for all you do, Deborah and Ken.

"Next to being married, a girl likes to be crossed in love a little now and then. It is something to think of and gives her a sort of distinction among her companions."

Jane Austen, *Pride and Prejudice*

CHAPTER 1

A CAPRICIOUS INDUCEMENT

KENT, ENGLAND - SPRING 1812

A sleepless night gave way to a pleasant morning. Miss Elizabeth Bennet quickly escaped the parsonage house for a solitary walk.

She could think of no better balm for all the tumult of her mind. The five weeks she had passed in Kent had made a noticeable difference, not only in the countryside—its trees and bushes growing lusher with each passing day—but to her equanimity as well. Surely her life would never be the same.

Thoughts of how she found herself in her current predicament accompanied her every step of the way.

Had my mother not insisted upon Jane going to Nether-

field Park on horseback, would the events of the past six months have unfolded differently?

Elizabeth would never have been subjected to such behavior on the part of her matchmaking mamma. Her fear of horses aside, Elizabeth was headstrong and unlikely to be made to do anything against her wishes.

Her sister Jane, on the other hand, was the kindest, most deferential person Elizabeth knew. It was not in her nature to disappoint anyone—especially her mother.

Had Jane ignored her mother's decree just that once, she would not have arrived at Netherfield during a rainstorm, and she would not have fallen ill. Elizabeth would not have gone there the next day to care for her. Her dearest sister for whom Elizabeth would do anything—including spurning the hand of the man who had offered a life of wealth and privilege. Mr. Fitzwilliam Darcy.

Had I not been forced to endure the proud Mr. Darcy's company for so long, surely he would not have persuaded himself that he loved me—against his reason according to his own words.

She scoffed. *As if I could ever be prevailed on to marry such a man—much less the man who has been the means of ruining the happiness of a most beloved sister.*

Elizabeth was on the point of continuing her walk

when she caught a glimpse of a gentleman within the sort of grove that edged the park. He was moving her way. Fearful of its being Mr. Darcy, she started retreating, but in vain, for the person who advanced was now near enough to see her and continued stepping forward with eagerness.

She had turned away, but on hearing herself called, though, in a voice that proved it to be Mr. Darcy's, she moved again toward the gate.

Anger and agitation accompanied Mr. Fitzwilliam Darcy every step of the way that morning. Determined to disabuse Miss Elizabeth Bennet of the unjust accusations she had leveled against him the evening before, he arose before the break of dawn and wrote in extensive detail in his defense.

Elizabeth's utter loathing of him had caught him completely by surprise. It would honor any woman in the country to be his wife—she would be a most fortunate creature indeed. Yet, she had allowed lies and misjudgments to guide her.

Why he had fallen in love with such a woman was beyond his reason. When he fell in love with her was just as perplexing. Surely it was not the first time he laid eyes on her at the Meryton assembly.

Only fools fall in love with such little provocation as a willing smile. As a testament against such a capricious inducement, he had declared her tolerable and unable to tempt him.

Perchance it was all the time spent in company with her at Netherfield that marked the start of his one-sided love affair. Her lovely dark, disheveled hair and her eyes, bright from the exertion of having walked three miles in the mud, nearly stole his breath away.

Her manner of rising to his every challenge during their many heated debates throughout the course of their days and nights under the same roof and the pleasure he received as a result equally baffled him.

Before too long, thoughts of her light and pleasing figure and her dark bewitching eyes wiped away every preconceived notion he held of what the ideal woman ought to be. He began to consider her as one of the handsomest women of his acquaintance.

I was in the middle of falling in love with Miss Elizabeth Bennet before I knew I had begun.

I fought against my better judgment and offered her my hand in marriage only to learn how much she disliked me—

how I was the last man in the world whom she could be prevailed on to marry.

Making matters worse, she had all but accused him of not being a gentleman. Her cold words echoed through his mind: *"You are mistaken, Mr. Darcy, if you suppose that the mode of your declaration affected me in any other way than as it spared me the concern I might have felt in refusing you had you behaved in a more gentlemanlike manner."*

After having delayed his departure from Kent several times with the thought of extending his courtship with Elizabeth, it had all been for naught. She hated him.

Darcy was on the point of continuing his walk when he caught a glimpse of the object of his fascination. He knew she would be there. Stepping forward with eagerness, he called out her name but to no avail, for she turned and walked away.

It would not do! After accusing him so egregiously, surely she owed it to him to hear his side of the story.

Still moving toward the gate, he called out once more.

"Miss Elizabeth Bennet!"

His hands clasped behind his back, a worn leather-bound tome folded in two and tucked snuggly in the pocket of his long black overcoat, William Collins ambled along the path. What a fine morning for a leisurely ramble. With such wonders of nature stretching before him, how could he not have conjured up what he supposed to be the perfect sermon for next Sunday's service?

Continuing his solitary trek, Collins silently congratulated himself on accomplishing a hard day's work. Nothing would pierce the morning's bliss.

Moments later, the fortunate young man of only five and twenty came to an abrupt halt. Every line of his mentally prepared sermon escaped his mind. Indeed, for just ahead in the lane stood Fitzwilliam Darcy, the distinguished young gentleman from Derbyshire and nephew of Collins's noble patroness, the Honorable Lady Catherine de Bourgh.

A fortuitous occasion indeed.

Collins arched his dark, bushy brow. *Had I known Mr. Darcy frequented this particular path, I would have traveled it more often.* His first inclination was to speed up his pace to greet the other man. He hesitated.

Mr. Darcy's agitated state appeared anything but welcoming. His pacing gave one to suspect he bore the weight of the world on his shoulder. Before Collins had too long to ponder what must weigh on Mr. Darcy's mind, someone else appeared from a distance. A young woman donned in a light muslin gown, a tan spencer, and a dark-colored bonnet.

Mr. Collins caught his breath. *Elizabeth!*

Elizabeth was a distant cousin whose acquaintance Collins had made several months prior. She was now a guest in his humble abode. He had his wife, Mrs. Charlotte Collins née Lucas, to thank for such a fate, owing to the two ladies being intimate friends.

Elizabeth bore the unhappy distinction of being headstrong and a bit imprudent in Collins's opinion. Despite his misgivings, he went along with the scheme to welcome Elizabeth into his home—his reasoning grounded in a peculiar self-satisfying concoction of gloating and spitefulness.

As a means of healing a long-standing breach in his family, Collins had ventured to Hertfordshire intending to choose a bride from among the five Bennet sisters, whose father's estate he stood next in line to inherit owing to an entail to the male line. Elizabeth had been his choice, but she spurned Collins's marriage proposal—a grave mistake on her part that he was unlikely to forgive and one he certainly would never forget.

Mr. Darcy's pacing ceased, and he approached

Elizabeth directly. From Collins's vantage point, his cousin looked as if she had been expecting the encounter.

Half appalled, half curious, he wondered aloud, "Is this the reason the young lady accepted my dear wife's invitation to visit us here in Kent?"

An even more shocking notion crossed his mind. *Is this the reason she refused to go to Rosings yesterday? Is this the reason Mr. Darcy fled the party soon after learning of Elizabeth's absence?*

The events leading up to Collins's proposal to his cousin and her steadfast rejection of his proposal took on new meaning. *This explains Mr. Darcy's singling out Miss Elizabeth at the Netherfield ball the evening before that fateful date.*

Collins's cautioning words to his cousin crossed his mind: *"My situation in life, my connections with the family of de Bourgh, and my relationship to your own are circumstances highly in my favor; and you should take it into further consideration that, in spite of your manifold attractions, it is by no means certain that another offer of marriage may ever be made you. Your portion is unhappily so small that it will, in all likelihood, undo the effects of your loveliness and amiable qualifications."*

His being a man of the cloth, the thought of spying on the couple was unconscionable. However, with his own reputation at stake, he could hardly turn a blind eye to such impropriety. Needing to be sure of what was unfolding before his eyes, Collins stooped down and, bolstered by a long stretch of hedgerows to shield his presence, eased a little closer. Though unable to hear what was being said, he saw Mr. Darcy extend his hand, bearing a missive of some sort. Making matters worse, Elizabeth accepted it with nary a moment's hesitation.

A young woman alone in the lane with a single young man was scandal-ridden in and of itself. Her accepting a letter from him—a man with whom she had no publicly acknowledged arrangement—was beyond the pale.

And this was the woman whom he had invited into his home. This woman whose propensity to flaunt proper decorum and who had so recently regarded his own noble patroness with such undignified impertinence had subjected both Collins and his dear wife to censure and shame.

Does she have no consideration for my standing in the community, my place among my parishioners?

He always knew his cousin to be a selfish person who only acted in accordance with her own interests. Her rejection of his marriage proposal was proof enough of that. He never supposed that her selfishness might be the means of his undoing—the loss of his esteem in the eyes of Lady Catherine and the world owing to such a connection.

Collins watched in wonder as Mr. Darcy bowed and walked away after Elizabeth accepted the letter. He could only speculate on what such behavior signified. Perhaps this brief encounter was merely the precursor to another rendezvous—some place more secluded.

Determined to find out, Collins trailed his cousin from a careful distance. He watched in wonder as she tore open the missive and read its contents. He thought he detected more vexation than pleasure in her countenance as she perused the pages.

Had Mr. Darcy written to put an end to their forbidden liaison? He was engaged to marry Miss Anne de Bourgh, after all. Collins knew this to be correct, for Lady Catherine always spoke of it as being the favorite wish of her family.

Collins did not know whether to feel sad for his cousin or glad for this turn of events. Had she not invited such heartbreak upon herself by aspiring to a station in life so far above her own as to be laughable?

Uneasiness washed over him. *This is no time to rejoice, for there still exists the possibility of Lady Catherine's learning of my cousin's brazenness.*

Upon following his cousin for almost an hour, Collins resolved to return to the parsonage. Soon enough, Elizabeth was bound to come back to the house as well.

To his manner of thinking, there was but one way to guarantee an agreeable outcome for himself in the wake of his cousin's scandalous behavior. He would be the one to inform his noble patroness. But first, he needed to get his hands on the letter that Mr. Darcy had given Elizabeth.

After reading Mr. Darcy's letter to my cousin, I shall know and understand precisely what I must do.

CHAPTER 2

A DISAGREEABLE CONNECTION

Just over a month after coming to Kent, Elizabeth was on her way back to London. However, unlike her arrival in that part of the country in the company of Sir William Lucas and his youngest daughter Mariah, Elizabeth now traveled alone. The gentleman returned to his home in Hertfordshire a week or so after his arrival. Mariah decided to remain in Kent for a lengthier visit with her sister, Charlotte.

Amid Charlotte's protests and even the Right Honorable Lady Catherine de Bourgh's, Elizabeth decided to leave Kent a week earlier than first planned.

So adamant was Lady Catherine to have her own way that she insisted Elizabeth remain in Kent until such time as her ladyship was to travel to London. There was no reason in the world why Elizabeth should not ride in the carriage with her ladyship, according to the grand lady's way of thinking. Then there would be no cause to put Elizabeth's uncle, Mr. Gardiner, through the trouble of conveying his niece to town.

Elizabeth shook her head in remembrance of the haughty aristocrat's benevolence. The last thing in the world Elizabeth wanted was to be beholden to such a woman. If there was any advantage in refusing Mr. Darcy's offer of marriage, it was that she had spared herself such a disagreeable connection.

No. Elizabeth was eager to be away from Kent—to be away from Lady Catherine. To be away from haunting memories of Mr. Darcy. To be away from her ridiculous cousin, Mr. Collins, whose behavior toward Elizabeth of late had become oddly discomforting, as though his opinion of her had soured.

Most of all, Elizabeth longed to reunite with her elder sister, Jane. Her last letter had hinted of a surprising reversal of fortune, one Jane dared not commit to writing for fear of spoiling it. To say Jane's missive was somewhat cryptic would have been an understatement but in a pleasant sort of way.

Not for the first time since receiving Jane's letter a

few days prior Elizabeth wondered at the source of her sister's revived spirits. Recollections of another missive could not help but intrude. The one Mr. Darcy handed her in the grove the morning he left Kent—specifically as it pertained to Jane and his friend, Mr. Charles Bingley.

Mr. Darcy.

Recalling the harsh words between them upon her learning the proud gentleman helped to separate the two lovers and his audacity to expect she would accept his hand despite it, Elizabeth shivered.

"And this is all the reply I am to have the honor of expecting! Perhaps, I might ask why, with so little endeavor at civility, I am thus rejected. But it is of small importance," he had opined.

To which Elizabeth replied, *"I might as well inquire why, with so evident a desire of offending and insulting me, you chose to tell me that you liked me against your will, against your reason, and even against your character? Was not this some excuse for incivility, if I was uncivil? But I have other provocations. You know I have.*

"Had not my feelings decided against you—had they been indifferent, or had they even been favorable, do you think that any consideration would tempt me to accept the man who has been the means of ruining, perhaps forever, the happiness of a most beloved sister?"

She recalled his expression on hearing her speak those words. Mr. Darcy changed color, but the emotion was short-lived, and he listened without attempting to interrupt her while she continued.

"I have every reason in the world to think ill of you. No motive can excuse the unjust and ungenerous part you acted there. You dare not, you cannot deny that you have been the principal if not the only means of dividing them from each other—of exposing one to the censure of the world for caprice and instability and the other to its derision for disappointed hopes and involving them both in misery of the acutest kind."

With no slight indignation, she had observed that he listened to her with an air that proved him wholly unmoved by any feeling of remorse. He even looked at her with a smile of affected incredulity, prompting her to inquire, *"Can you deny that you have done it?"*

With assumed tranquility, he then responded, *"I have no wish of denying that I did everything in my power to separate my friend from your sister or that I rejoice in my success. Toward him, I have been kinder than toward myself."*

Were Elizabeth to rely on Mr. Darcy's letter, she would never suspect he had a part to play in a possible reunion between Jane and Mr. Bingley. The specific passage belying that possibility came to mind:

Perhaps this concealment, this disguise, was beneath me. It is done, however, and it was done for the best. On this subject, I have nothing more to say, no other apology to offer. If I have wounded your sister's feelings, it was unknowingly done. Though the motives which governed me may to you very naturally appear insufficient, I have not yet learned to condemn them.

In truth, the events that unfolded prior to his leave-taking fueled her hopes. Immediately upon returning from her hours-long ramble about the park, Elizabeth received word from Charlotte that she had missed the morning's visitors.

Lady Catherine's nephews had called during her absence. Mr. Darcy stayed only for a few minutes, but his cousin Colonel Fitzwilliam had been sitting with them at least an hour, hoping for Elizabeth's return.

With his letter's contents weighing heavy on her mind, Elizabeth could only suppose that indeed Mr. Darcy must bear no ill will toward her. *How else is his coming to the parsonage to be explained? What must a man of Mr. Darcy's temperament care about slighting the Collinses by not calling on them before taking his leave of Kent?*

Her heart could not help but whisper he had done it for her, just as she now understood his every visit to the parsonage implicitly had been to see her. Their every seemingly coincidental encounter in the lanes had been by his design.

Is it too much to hope that for my sake, if nothing else, Mr. Darcy sought to redress the harm he caused my sister?

Elizabeth picked up her book and flipped through the pages, hoping to divert her busy mind away from thoughts of Mr. Darcy and suppositions of what he may or may not have done. All in vain.

You must allow me to tell you how ardently I admire and love you.

However repulsed Elizabeth might have been upon first hearing Mr. Darcy's ardent avowal, she would be lying if she denied his words now meant something to her, even if she was sure she might never hear them again and even if she was unsure whether she might ever wish to.

Thoughts of Jane's letter intruded once again, specifically the part that read, *I do not dare commit my reversal of fortune to paper, thinking as I do that fate is a fickle friend at best. For now, I will only say my happiness is almost complete.*

Staring out the window at the countryside and admiring the abounding sights of spring as far as the eyes could see whisking by, Elizabeth sighed. *Barring any travel delays, soon, my dearest Jane and I will be together again. Until such time as I can adequately satisfy my curiosity, I shall think no more on the matter.*

Elizabeth's carriage drove to the Gardiners' door at the appointed time. The scene was much the same as she remembered it some weeks earlier when she had arrived from Hertfordshire with the Lucases with Jane sitting in the drawing room window awaiting her arrival. When she entered the passage, Jane welcomed Elizabeth with open arms and a smile as bright as the younger sister could ever wish to see.

Elizabeth glanced to the top of the stairs with the expectation of seeing a troop of little boys and girls, eager for attention from an older cousin. They were nowhere around, giving Elizabeth to suspect they were likely away at the nearby park. It was just as well, for Elizabeth's primary design was the reunion with her sister and the unraveling of the mystery Jane's letter had wrought.

Sitting beside her sister in the drawing room, Elizabeth said, "Dearest Jane, I cannot tell you how pleased I am seeing you looking so lovely. Pray, I am not speaking out of turn in saying it is most refreshing in comparison to when I was here last." She took Jane by the hand. "Dare I say it is attributable to the change in circumstances you alluded to in your last letter?"

Jane blushed crimson. Despite her modesty, her natural beauty could not help but shine through.

"I would have to say it has everything to do with it," she replied. "Oh, Lizzy! It has been so long since I had reason to feel as hopeful as I do."

Indeed, Jane's melancholy had persisted for months. Elizabeth feared the combination of Mr. Bingley's defection and his sister Miss Caroline Bingley's betrayal of what Jane had supposed was genuine affection between them jaded Jane's wont to only see the best in people. This picture of her elder sister warmed Elizabeth's heart. She squeezed her sister's hand. "Pray, do not keep me in suspense."

Jane was about to say more when both she and Elizabeth were suddenly roused by the sound of the doorbell. Jane's face overspread with joy, as though she was expecting someone to call.

Releasing her sister's hand, Elizabeth's breath caught. She jumped to her feet.

Any number of thoughts raced through her head, the most unsettling of them all having to do with her suspicion that Jane's newfound happiness indeed had to do with a renewal of her acquaintance with Mr. Bingley and the possibility that Mr. Darcy had been the means of bringing it about.

Jane stood and smoothed her skirt. Elizabeth also adjusted her attire.

The thought that not only was Mr. Bingley the imminent guest but that Mr. Darcy might be accompanying him also crossed her mind. Before she had time to think about what such a prospect must portend, the door of the drawing room opened, and in walked the Gardiners' housekeeper with two gentlemen on her heels.

CHAPTER 3

VERY AGREEABLE STRANGERS

Until that moment, Elizabeth had not realized how much she was depending on the gentleman caller being Mr. Bingley; more than that, how much she was hoping the other gentleman would be Mr. Darcy. Her heart sank. Then her eyes fell on Jane, whose eyes were full of joy.

Elizabeth did not hear the Gardiners' housekeeper present the visitors—at least not clearly. Her busy mind was frantically engaged in conjecture and speculation of how she could have been so wrong. Before she knew what she was about, the housekeeper had retreated from the drawing room and she and Jane sat opposite two very agreeable strangers.

When the gentlemen were gone, Elizabeth said, "Jane, you are very sly. Not once did you mention your having met Mr. Hemmingsworth in your letters to me while I was in Kent."

"Dearest Lizzy," Jane began, her voice filled with more joyfulness than contrition, "pray you will forgive me. Not that I did not want to tell you. I just did not know how to tell you."

"Whatever does that mean, Jane?" Elizabeth asked. "You realize you can tell me anything."

Jane nodded. "I do, but I feared if I spoke of my new acquaintance, you might think of me as being capricious."

"Do you mean regarding your affection for Mr. Bingley?"

"You always thought his feelings for me were greater than I did. I did not wish to disappoint you."

"I am sorry I caused you to feel you could not share your budding feelings for Mr. Hemmingsworth with me. I should have liked to have known."

Elizabeth spoke nothing but the truth in saying that. Part of her ill feelings toward Mr. Darcy had to do with his role in separating Jane and his friend Mr. Bingley. Elizabeth recalled having argued to him that Jane's attachment to Mr. Bingley was strong, even though Mr. Darcy had stated that he had detected no such sentiments on Jane's part.

Is it possible that I may have been mistaken? Jane,

herself, had suggested an attachment between Mr. Bingley and her evidently was not meant to be despite my observations to the contrary.

Was I wrong to attribute my sister's sentiments as her way of protecting her broken heart? I, better than anyone, understand Jane's penchant to hide her true feelings from everyone. Only those who know her best have an inkling of what she is feeling.

On the other hand, I cannot deny the events that have just unfolded.

Based on all Elizabeth observed, Jane was very fond of Mr. Hemmingsworth. Not only did her elder sister smile a lot, but she also laughed. Elizabeth told her sister as much. She asked when and how the two of them met.

"Oh, you will never believe the odd confluence of events that led to my meeting him. Ironically, there is a connection to Mr. Bingley himself."

"Mr. Bingley?" Elizabeth asked, her voice a mixture of intrigue and concern. "What does your meeting Mr. Hemmingsworth have to do with Mr. Bingley?"

"Well, just over a fortnight ago, while I was attending the theater with our aunt and uncle, I espied Mr. Bingley."

"You did? Why did you not mention this in your letters? Did the two of you have a chance to speak?"

Jane shook her head. "We did not. I was sitting in the lower level, and I noticed him high above in one of the private boxes. Of course, he could not have seen me. It appears the young lady seated next to him was all that caught his eye. The prospect of it all was a bit too much for me to bear.

"I excused myself from my party and hastened into the lobby. Not paying attention to where I was going, I collided with Mr. Hemmingsworth." Jane covered her mouth with her hand to hide her smile. "Oh! Lizzy, I have never been more embarrassed in all my life, so much so I burst into tears."

Elizabeth's own smile widened. "And then what happened?"

"I am afraid things only got worse, for he was holding a drink in his hand–a burgundy wine, no less. I caused him to spill his drink on his crisp white cravat. Aghast, I somehow retrieved a handkerchief from my purse, and I started dabbing spilled wine from his cravat, which undoubtedly made it worse. Fortunately, there was no one around to observe my impetuous behavior."

Jane's composure grew uncharacteristically animated. She continued, "I knew not what I was about until he took my hand in his and leaned closer."

Elizabeth's eyes opened wide. Albeit amused, she stayed silent.

"He then took the handkerchief from me. He said, 'If you continue to go on in this way, someone is bound to think you are my wife.'"

Jane blushed a little.

Elizabeth could honestly say she had not seen her sister so lively in what seemed like years. She liked seeing Jane this way. She really did.

Elizabeth wanted to know more about Jane's budding relationship with this new acquaintance. The last time she saw Jane, Elizabeth was sure her sister was head over heels in love with Mr. Charles Bingley and was suffering a broken heart because of his defection.

It seemed that Jane had moved on and rather quickly at that, which posed a conundrum for Elizabeth. Part of her reason for refusing Mr. Darcy's hand in marriage was because of Jane's disappointed hopes and his role in causing it.

Elizabeth loved her sister very much, and she wanted her to be happy. She decided to support her and find out more about this promising relationship with someone new.

"What did you say?" Elizabeth cried.

"I offered a heartfelt apology, and I begged his

forgiveness. At which point he said he would forgive me on but one condition—that I must tell him my name."

"How scandalous!" Elizabeth exclaimed half-jokingly, half-seriously. "And then what happened?"

"What else could I do but curtsey and hurry away? I returned to my seat as fast as I could only to find, a little later, that he had followed me, or at least that is what I thought at the time, when all along he was seated directly behind me—he and his brother. For a moment, I thought I was seeing double." Jane laughed a little. "Oh, Lizzy, do you not agree that Mr. Hemmingsworth and his brother are two of the most handsome men you have ever seen?"

Elizabeth dared not argue her sister's point. The two gentlemen were very good-looking indeed—tall, dark, and handsome with dark curls and arresting eyes. Everything about their appearance gave much to admire. What was more, the gentlemen were most congenial.

Were I to guess, I would say they are aged four and twenty, perhaps a little older, but certainly not as old as Mr. Darcy, she further considered in silence.

Still, there was a seriousness about the gentlemen that belied their youth. It amazed Elizabeth the ease with which she and the younger brother fell into conversation while Jane spoke with the older.

This characterization of the older versus the younger caused Elizabeth to chuckle inside. The gentlemen had jokingly referred to themselves in those terms, what with their being twins born mere minutes apart. The brotherly affection they shared was evident. Why, they even completed each other's sentences. The older of the two bore the name Stanford and the younger Mitchell.

"Jane, that is an interesting initial meeting to be sure. As much as I want to know more, I cannot be satisfied entirely until you tell me what became of Mr. Bingley. Did the two of you ever come face-to-face that night?"

"No," Jane said, her voice bearing a slight hint of regret. "I cannot say with certainty what became of Mr. Bingley after that. I am afraid my mind was more agreeably engaged with thoughts of Mr. Hemmingsworth for the rest of the evening."

For Elizabeth's part, a hint of disappointment could not be repressed. She had been absolutely persuaded of her sister's love for Mr. Bingley for so long, perhaps to her own detriment.

Sensing this, Jane cried, "Now, Lizzy, surely you cannot be too disappointed in my saying that. It has been months since Mr. Bingley left Hertfordshire with the promise of returning. Months. You cannot expect me to pine away for him forever."

"Jane, are you saying you no longer have any feelings at all for Mr. Bingley?"

"No—I am not saying that. What I am saying is that when and if he and I ever do come face-to-face again, I am sure we shall meet as little more than indifferent acquaintances."

Elizabeth exhaled a deep sigh in resignation. "If you say so, I have no other choice than to believe you."

"I say so."

The younger woman half-smiled. "And here you are weeks later, receiving a morning call from the gentleman and his brother. Tell me, has he called often since making your acquaintance?"

"Yes, he has," Jane confessed. "He has even dined here at my uncle's behest. They have several mutual acquaintances in business. However, today was the first time his brother joined him. I believe I owe that particular courtesy to you."

"Me?" Elizabeth asked.

"Indeed, for I might have mentioned to Mr. Hemmingsworth that you were due to arrive from Kent," Jane said smilingly.

"Pray, do not tell me you have taken on the role of playing matchmaker, dearest Jane."

"Well," Jane began, "he is a single man in possession of a good fortune. I can only suppose he must be in want of a wife."

Elizabeth said, "That makes two single men with good fortunes in want of wives, does it not?"

Jane smiled. Placing her finger on her chin, she said, "I suppose I never really thought about that."

"Heaven forbid. No one who knows you best would ever think of you as being mercenary."

Jane scoffed. "No one other than Miss Caroline Bingley, that is."

"Oh, let us not spoil this happy moment with thoughts of that miserable woman," Elizabeth said. "I am much more interested in continuing our discussion of the Hemmingsworth brothers."

Elizabeth then leaned closer to her sister. "You mentioned the gentlemen having good fortunes. Pray, tell me, how wealthy are the Hemmingsworths?"

"Lizzy!" Jane exclaimed.

"What? Let us not pretend that is not the first question our mother will ask once she finds out about them. I simply want to know what I ought to say."

CHAPTER 4

A MOMENT'S REFLECTION

*D*arcy looked up upon espying his friend Charles Bingley enter the room. It had been ages since they last saw each other. For a while, they had kept in touch by way of letters. That was before Darcy's disastrous proposal to Miss Elizabeth Bennet. Since then, he had cut himself off from almost everyone.

"I had expected your return to town weeks ago." Taking a seat, Bingley sank contentedly into the finely upholstered chair.

Situated on the opposite side of his large mahogany desk, Darcy set aside the book he had been reading. "Indeed, but I traveled to Somersetshire rather than come directly to London."

"In your last letter, you mentioned Miss Elizabeth

being in Kent visiting her friend, Mrs. Collins. Did you have occasion to spend time in each other's company?"

"Numerous occasions, in fact," Darcy said.

"Did she happen to ask about me? I suppose she must wonder about my failure to return to Hertfordshire as I had promised."

Did she ever, Darcy considered. Much to his chagrin, his deliberate interference in his friend and her sister's relationship had been the catalyst for his most heated debate with Elizabeth ever—the one in which she rejected his offer of marriage.

"She did," Darcy said, hoping he would not have to say more.

"You would not believe this, but I could swear I have seen Miss Bennet here in town—on many occasions, in fact. At the theater, at a shop in Mayfair, and at one time on a crowded street. I always supposed it was just my imagination running away with me. Surely, were Miss Bennet in town, she would have made her presence known to me."

"Actually, it may not have been your imagination at all. Miss Bennet is in town—at least she was here in town visiting her relations in Cheapside. I do not know if she remains in town."

"What! Did Miss Elizabeth tell you her sister was in town?"

Darcy nodded.

"And you thought to keep this information to yourself?" Bingley pounded his fist on Darcy's desk, disrupting a stack of papers. "Can you explain your reasoning?"

Explain my reasoning? Darcy considered while watching his suddenly emboldened friend nurse his aching hand. *Since when have I sought to explain my motives to anyone?*

Since I wrote a lengthy letter trying to explain myself to Miss Elizabeth Bennet, his broken heart whispered. Would he ever forget the pain of having to write such a letter? To that day, its opening paragraph weighed heavily on his mind.

"Be not alarmed, madam, on receiving this letter, by the apprehension of its containing any repetition of those sentiments or renewal of those offers that were last night so disgusting to you. I write without any intention of paining you or humbling myself by dwelling on wishes that cannot be too soon forgotten for the happiness of both. The effort which the formation and the perusal of this letter must occasion should have been spared had not my character required it to be written and read. You must, therefore, pardon the freedom with which I demand your attention.

Your feelings, I know, will bestow it unwillingly, but I demand it of your justice."

Never before had he bared his innermost thoughts to anyone. Only Elizabeth had garnered in him so much trust. He prayed he would never have cause to regret such openness on his part.

Feigning indifference toward Bingley's uncharacteristic outburst, Darcy shrugged. "I am telling you now, am I not?"

Bingley sprang from his seat and started pacing the floor. "It has been months since Miss Bennet and I saw each other. The last words I spoke to her were the promise of my imminent return." He looked at Darcy. "Do you think she will forgive me? Do you think I stand a chance of reclaiming all that I might have lost of her affection?"

Busy tidying up his desk, Darcy said, "I am happy to accompany you to Cheapside to call on Miss Bennet if you think it will help."

"You would really do that for me?" Bingley asked, his countenance overtaken with hope.

"Of course I will. What are friends for?" he asked, not exactly letting on he had his own motives for wanting to go with his friend. No one knew how deeply in love with Elizabeth he had been all that time in Hertfordshire. She had bewitched him like no other woman he had ever known, and not even the sting of her harsh rebuke had released him from her spell. If there was a chance to see her—even if for the last time, he would take it.

Darcy nodded in response to Bingley's question.

"But why? Not that I do not appreciate the gesture, but I know how fastidious you are. I should imagine hardly a month's ablution enough to cleanse you from its impurities were you to enter that particular part of town."

After a moment's reflection, Bingley continued, "That is unless you wish to observe Miss Bennet and me together to make sure of her attachment. Is that it? Because if it is, then I will have to decline your offer. Going forward, I shall follow my own counsel where it concerns Miss Bennet."

"As you should," Darcy said.

"If that is not your reason, then pray tell me what is." A hint of understanding flashed before Bingley's eyes. "Unless your wanting to go there is because of Miss Elizabeth."

"My reasoning has everything to do with Miss Elizabeth," Darcy conceded. "I finally came to realize just how much she meant to me," he confessed to his friend. "Indeed, I told her as much when the two of us were in Kent."

Of course, Darcy dared not tell his friend that he had proposed to Elizabeth and she flatly rejected his proposal without a second thought. In this matter, he too would keep his own counsel.

"It was to no avail," Darcy said in response to his friend's stunned silence. "I came to know she had a dreadfully unfavorable opinion of me."

He recoiled on the inside in recollection of Elizabeth's words: *"From the very beginning—from the first moment, I may almost say—of my acquaintance with you, your manners, impressing me with the fullest belief of your arrogance, your conceit, and your selfish disdain of the feelings of others, were such as to form the groundwork of disapprobation on which succeeding events have built so immovable a dislike, and I had not known you a month before I felt that you were the last man in the world whom I could ever be prevailed on to marry."*

"I fear our manner of parting ways in Kent left much to be desired. I should like the chance to make amends," said Darcy.

"Well then," Bingley stated, "of course you must come." Then, unable to keep the broad smile from spreading across his face, he asked, "When shall we go? Now that I know Jane is here in town, I cannot stand the thought of us being apart a moment longer than necessary."

"I hate to dampen your enthusiasm, but I am afraid you will have to wait until tomorrow. It would be highly inappropriate to call on anyone at this hour, especially with this being your first meeting with the Bennets' London relations. Of course, that is assuming Miss Bennet is still in town, for she very well may have returned to Hertfordshire by now."

This thought pained Darcy, for if Miss Bennet were no longer in London, the same would likely go for Elizabeth. Who was to say when or if he would ever see her again?

"Not only that," Darcy said, willing away his melancholy, "did you not insist upon my accompanying you to the theater this evening? We made this plan months ago."

The last thing in the world Darcy wanted to be doing that evening was attending the theater, especially during that time of year, when eager mammas as far as the eyes could see would be promoting their simpering daughters before men with sizable fortunes. He did not have the heart to turn his friend Bingley down. As heartbroken as Bingley still was over Miss Jane Bennet, at least the younger man was out in society trying to put on a good face.

Being partially to blame for Bingley's disappointed hopes, attending the theater with him was the least he could do, especially since Bingley was availing himself of Darcy's private box. The theater, however, was where he meant to draw the line. Darcy was certain he would not be attending balls and private dinner parties and the like. He was, after all, nursing his own wounded heart and disappointed hopes—even if he was the only one who knew it.

"I did indeed. And, of course, you are correct. For the sake of propriety, my reunion with Miss Bennet will have to wait until tomorrow." Bingley flashed a broad smile—one Darcy could not help but notice.

"What are you thinking, Charles?"

"I am meditating on the possibility that Miss Bennet might be in attendance at the theater this evening."

A bit of hope crept into Darcy's mind at hearing this. *Should both Bennet sisters be in attendance, it would be an interesting prospect indeed.*

That night, at the theater, Jane made an excuse of wanting to refresh herself. She really hoped to free herself from the unease she suffered in espying Mr. Charles Bingley. She had only caught a glimpse of him before he disappeared into the crowd, but she was sure it was him. She would recognize his striking mane among a thousand men.

The last thing she expected was to see him in the lobby. But there he was, standing nearby a column. Searching. Waiting.

Had he seen her as well? Was he looking for her?

I must compose myself. I simply must. I am here with Mr. Hemmingsworth as his mother's guest. Mr. Bingley is part of my history.

Her heart pounded. Maybe an accidental encounter with Mr. Bingley was just what Jane had been hoping for—the reason she had escaped her party in the first place. Or maybe not.

It is too much. It is too soon, Jane considered, even though her very reason for being in town had been to reunite with Mr. Bingley.

His pernicious sisters' behavior all but dealt a death blow to Jane's scheme. Her feelings being anything but indifferent, as she had hoped, Jane determined to strike a different path than the one that was sure to bring her face-to-face with the past.

"Miss Bennet? Is that you?" Jane heard someone ask.

Jane turned to identify the speaker. She forced a smile to her face. "Mr. Hurst," she said, curtseying.

"Well—well, it is you! It has been far too long since

my eyes suffered the pleasure of beholding so much beauty."

"You are very kind, sir."

"I say nothing that is not true." He raised his monocle to his eye and indeed beheld Jane from head to toe.

She could feel the color spread all over her body. She always knew the gentleman to be licentious. Still, she rather supposed his propensity was reserved for food and drink.

"My brother-in-law, Bingley, is also in attendance this evening. No doubt he will want to see you." Mr. Hurst offered Jane his arm. "Shall the two of us go in search of him?"

"Miss Bennet?"

Looking just over Hurst's shoulder, Jane noticed another gentleman heading her way. Mr. Charles Bingley.

There really is no escaping him now.

Mr. Hurst lowered his arm and stepped aside to make room for Bingley. "Here you are, Brother. I just invited Miss Bennet to go in search of you."

Bingley swallowed. "Miss Bennet," he said, his voice a half-broken whisper.

Her composure no less disturbed than his, Jane thought to extend her gloved hand, but she did not. It was far too bold a gesture. She clutched either side of her gown and curtsied instead. "Mr. Bingley."

His tone conveying something of real regret, Bingley said, "It is a very long time since I have had the pleasure of seeing you."

Before Jane could reply, he added, "It is above six months. We have not met since the twenty-sixth of November when we were all dancing together at Netherfield."

Jane was pleased to find his memory so exact. If only he had remembered to keep his promise to return to Netherfield after he concluded his business in town some three days hence. Jane was sure she did not wish to discuss the matter at that moment.

Trapped in an awkward engagement with two gentlemen was not Jane's idea of how she ought to be comporting herself that evening. Then Mr. Stanford Hemmingsworth joined the party. He offered Jane the beverage he was holding.

"Thank you, sir," she said, accepting his proffered drink. "How did you know I was in need of refreshment?"

Tucking both hands behind his back, the handsome gentleman stood straight and tall. "I like to think the business of my life is anticipating your needs, Miss Bennet."

Smiling, Jane tore her eyes away from Hemmingsworth's long enough to take a sip of her drink. A familiar stirring deep inside overtook her, and soon enough, she gazed into Hemmingsworth's eyes again.

Mr. Bingley cleared his throat, summoning Jane's attention as well as Hemmingsworth's.

"Friends of yours from Hertfordshire, I presume?"

"Yes," Jane began, "well, actually, no." A bit flustered, she said, "Allow me to introduce you." Gesturing to the elder of the two, she said, "Mr. Hurst, Mr. Bingley, this is Mr. Hemmingsworth." Before any of the gentlemen could muster the usual civilities, Jane said, "Mr. Bingley resides here in town—that is to say he was, or rather he is, my neighbor in Hertfordshire. His estate abuts my father's. Mr. Hurst is Mr. Bingley's brother-in-law. He also resides here in town."

Hemmingsworth said, "Mr. Hurst, Mr. Bingley, it is my pleasure. I have heard good things about Hertfordshire. I understand there is so much to entertain. I too am thinking of acquiring property there."

"I am sure you would find it to be a lovely place," Bingley said. "I have no complaints." He looked at Jane and continued, "I miss everything about it."

His words drew Jane's eyes to his. Neither seemed

capable of looking away. His words were so simple yet so eloquently put. Jane was surely affected.

"How could you not?" Mr. Hemmingsworth asked, directing his inquiry pointedly to Mr. Bingley. "I shall consider your words as a wholehearted endorsement." The gentleman extended his arm to Jane. "Shall I escort you inside? My mother must not worry over our long absence."

CHAPTER 5

A CASUAL ACQUAINTANCE

Concerned about what could be keeping Jane, Elizabeth had also escaped the party. The lobby was more crowded than she had expected. She did not wander about long before espying Mr. Darcy. She only caught a glimpse of him, for he was heading to a different part of the theater. A single glimpse was all it took, for Elizabeth would have recognized his noble mien among a thousand men.

This was but the second time seeing the gentleman since refusing his offer of marriage. It was the first time seeing him since suffering something akin to regret. Would she have refused him had she known what she now knew having committed his letter to heart?

The two offenses she accused him of she had by

now forgiven him for. What was there not to forgive? In separating Jane and Bingley, he had been acting in service of his friend. In confiding his family's harrowing secret, he had proved Elizabeth's former favorite, a Mr. George Wickham, to be the scoundrel he indeed was. But the cold, ungentlemanly manner in which he offered his hand and the stern criticism of her family—he had done nothing to assuage her dislike in either of those two respects. She could have no reason to think he ever would.

Still, Elizabeth could scarcely deny having longed to see the gentleman upon first returning to London from Kent. She had hoped to see him in company with his friend Bingley—calling on Jane in Cheapside—as his way of making amends for his interference.

He never came.

"Miss Eliza Bennet? Is that you?" Elizabeth heard someone ask.

Elizabeth turned to identify the speaker. She forced a smile to her face. "Mrs. Hurst, Miss Bingley," she said, curtseying.

"Well—well, it is you! For a moment, I thought my eyes were deceiving me," said Miss Bingley, the younger and the most pernicious of the two Bingley sisters.

"You act as though it surprises you to see me here

in London. It is not as though you were unaware of Jane's being here. She told me she visited you soon after she arrived in town."

"Yes, well, that was ages ago. I surely thought our dear Miss Bennet would have returned to Hertfordshire by now. Is she here tonight as well?"

Trapped in an awkward engagement with two of her least favorite people in the world was not exactly Elizabeth's idea of how she ought to be spending her time that evening.

"She is indeed," Elizabeth said. "If you will pardon me, I am looking for her."

"Pray do not hurry off on our account, Miss Eliza," said Miss Bingley. She seized Elizabeth's arm in hers and silently coaxed her sister into doing the same. "I say we join you in looking for Miss Bennet. No doubt a lovely reunion awaits us all."

The ladies did not walk far before being arrested by none other than Mr. Darcy. The Bingley sisters released Elizabeth's arms and snatched his without a second's hesitation. He not too subtly wrenched himself free.

"Miss Elizabeth," he said, bowing.

"Mr. Darcy," Elizabeth said.

Not to be denied her fair share of Mr. Darcy's attention, Miss Bingley said, "Is this not a lovely surprise, Mr. Darcy? We have not had the pleasure of Miss Eliza's company in months." She looked at Elizabeth. "Did I not promise you a lovely reunion for us all? A long overdue one at that, for our Mr. Darcy only recently returned to town himself."

"Oh?" Elizabeth heard herself ask.

"Indeed, Miss Elizabeth. After I left Kent, I traveled to Somersetshire."

"At this time of year, during the height of the London season, no less. What on earth were you thinking of staying away from all of your friends for so long?" Miss Bingley cried.

Mr. Darcy flashed an annoyed glance at Miss Bingley. "After my stay in Kent, I needed some time away from everything." He looked longingly at Elizabeth. "Not that it made a great difference. And you, Miss Elizabeth—how long has it been since you took your leave of Kent?"

"A few weeks," Elizabeth said, a bit confused by his gentle tone. Perhaps he was not as disappointed in her as she thought he would be—not that it mattered if he were. She was just as much an injured party as he was, after all. Her uncivil refusal was perfectly in keeping with his insulting proposal.

That harrowing evening's events still lingered in her mind. Mr. Darcy spoke well, but there were feelings besides those of the heart to be detailed, and he was no more eloquent on the subject of tenderness than of pride. His sense of her inferiority—of its being a degradation—of the family obstacles which had always opposed to inclination, were dwelt on with a warmth which seemed due to the consequence he was wounding but was very unlikely to recommend his suit.

As much as she did not wish to dwell on the past, there was one part of his proposal that accompanied Elizabeth to sleep each night.

You must allow me to tell you how ardently I admire and love you.

Elizabeth could not repress her heart's whispering, *Does Mr. Darcy still love me?*

"Kent!" Miss Bingley exclaimed. "Do you mean to say the two of you were together in Kent?"

Before either Elizabeth or Mr. Darcy could fashion a reply, Mr. Mitchell Hemmingsworth joined their party.

He offered Elizabeth the beverage he was holding.

"Thank you, sir," she said, accepting his proffered drink. "How did you know I was in need of refreshment?"

Tucking both hands behind his back, the handsome gentleman stood straight and tall. "Part of the joy of becoming better acquainted with you these past weeks is learning to anticipate your needs, Miss Elizabeth."

Elizabeth lowered her eyes and raised her glass to her lips. She took a long sip. *Mr. Hemmingsworth, you are positively incorrigible,* she thought but did not voice aloud. The last thing she wanted was to have Mr. Darcy believe she was flirting with some other gentleman on the heels of rejecting his proposal because—because…

Elizabeth raised her eyes and gazed into Mr. Hemmingsworth's. His eyes shone with amusement. Mr. Darcy cleared his throat, summoning Elizabeth's attention as well as Hemmingsworth's.

"Friends of yours from Hertfordshire, I presume?"

"Yes," Elizabeth began, "well, actually, no." A bit flustered, she said, "Allow me to introduce you." Gesturing to the elder of the three, she said, "Mr. Darcy, Mrs. Hurst, Miss Bingley, this is Mr. Hemmingsworth."

Before anyone could muster the usual civilities, Elizabeth said, "Mr. Darcy's friend, Mr. Bingley, resides here in town—that is to say he was, or he is, my neighbor in Hertfordshire. His estate abuts my father's. Mrs. Hurst and Miss Bingley are Mr. Bingley's sisters. They also reside here in town."

Hemmingsworth said, "Mr. Darcy, Mrs. Hurst, and

Miss Bingley, it is my pleasure. From all I have heard about Hertfordshire, there is much to entertain. I am looking forward to discovering it all for myself."

"I am sure you would find it to be a lovely place," Mr. Darcy said. He looked at Elizabeth and continued, "I am sure I shall cherish my time spent in that part of the country for the rest of my life."

His words drew Elizabeth's eyes to his. Neither seemed capable of looking away. For Elizabeth's part, what she saw in Mr. Darcy's eyes was admiration—perhaps even love.

You must allow me to tell you how ardently I admire and love you.

Was she only seeing what she wanted to see? How could that be? Why would that be?

"How could you not?" Mr. Hemmingsworth asked, directing his inquiry pointedly to Mr. Darcy. "I shall consider your words as a wholehearted endorsement." The gentleman extended his arm to Elizabeth. "Shall I escort you inside the theater? My mother and your sister must not worry over our long absence."

A quarter-hour after Mr. Darcy finished his cognac, his friend Charles Bingley waltzed into White's looking equally downtrodden. He headed directly to Darcy's table and pulled up a chair.

"It appears the play was not to your liking either," said Darcy, signaling the waiter.

"The play?" Bingley asked.

"Yes—the play," Darcy began, "the one the two of us attended earlier this evening."

When the waiter approached, Bingley ordered a double whiskey. Before the waiter had gone away, he said, "On second thought, bring the whole bottle, please. Make that two bottles!"

"Charles, what on earth has gotten into you?"

"Oh, Darcy! I believe this has been the worst night of my life. You will never guess who I saw at the theater this evening—on the arm of another man."

"Miss Jane Bennet?"

"How did you know? Did you know my Jane was going to be there on the arm of another? Is that why you were so easily persuaded to accompany me?"

"No—I would not deliberately subject you to such harsh treatment. Despite what you must be thinking of me, I have never meant to cause you any harm."

"Then how did you know I was speaking of Jane?"

"I saw Miss Bennet's eldest sister at the theater." He silently scoffed. *Is that what Elizabeth and I are to each other now?* he considered. *She is Miss Bennet's eldest sister, and I am merely Mr. Bingley's friend.* He tightened his grip on his glass in remembrance of the nonchalant manner of her earlier introduction to her gentleman acquaintance. "Miss Elizabeth," he said. He tossed back his drink, thinking how prescient of Bingley to order two bottles. *She too was on the arm of another man.*

"If you could have seen Miss Bennet and the pompous gentleman who approached us while we were in the middle of our conversation and purposely swept her away as if she were his," Bingley complained.

"Perhaps you imagined things, Charles," said Darcy, as though he were trying to convince himself that the gentleman who swooped in and swept Elizabeth away was no more than a casual acquaintance.

"If only that were true. I fear I know Jane too well to suppose the gentleman meant nothing to her. He had the audacity to say the business of his life was anticipating her needs."

Darcy almost choked in remembrance of hearing words of a similar vein himself. *"Part of the joy of becoming better acquainted with you these past weeks is learning to anticipate your needs, Miss Elizabeth."*

Darcy scoffed. "Did the man actually say that?"

Bingley nodded. "He further insinuated his plans to acquire property in Hertfordshire."

Darcy frowned. The disturbance of his composure was increasing by the second.

"From all I have heard about Hertfordshire, there is much to entertain. I am looking forward to discovering it all for myself."

The similarities between Darcy's chance encounter with Elizabeth and Bingley's chance encounter with Miss Bennet were too unsettling for his taste.

"Then he led Jane away with some excuse of not wanting his mother to worry," Bingley said.

This was too much. "Did this gentleman have a name?" Darcy asked.

Bingley ran his fingers through his hair. "I believe it was Hemsley—no Hemsworth—no Hemms—"

"Hemmingsworth?" Darcy interrupted; his brow arched.

Bingley shook his finger in the air. "Yes—Hemmingsworth. But—but how could you possibly have guessed? Do you know of a Mr. Hemmingsworth?"

"I do now," Darcy said.

"Now?"

"Yes. As of tonight, to be exact. Miss Elizabeth and I were standing together, having a reunion of our own

—of sorts, when a gentleman approached us from out of nowhere. She introduced him as a Mr. Hemmingsworth."

"Who is this man?" Bingley asked, slamming his glass on the table. "Where did he come from? And most importantly, what is his connection to the Bennets?"

"That I cannot say. But there is one way to find out."

"Do you mean to hire a private investigator to look into the matter?"

"I suppose if it comes to that. However, there is an easier way to unravel this mystery."

"Pray, do not keep me in suspense."

"Bingley, did we not plan to call on Miss Bennet in Cheapside on the morrow?"

The younger man lowered his head. He lowered his voice. "After what I witnessed tonight, I fear I might be too late."

Perhaps it contented Bingley to let things be with the woman he professed to be in love with. It was not in Darcy's nature to do so. "Bingley, it may or may not be too late. If Miss Bennet means half as much to you as you say she does, do you not owe it to yourself to find out all you can?"

Hours later, in Cheapside, the Bennet sisters were lying in their beds, both too excited to sleep.

"You and your Mr. Hemmingsworth are getting on very well, Jane. I dare say you will miss him greatly when we return to Hertfordshire."

"I dare say I will at that. However, I have good reason to believe it will not be long before we are reunited."

"Oh?"

"Indeed—though I cannot say too much on the subject at this time."

"For fear of inviting trouble?"

"Let me just say I am more than a little encouraged by the prospect."

"I would say at the speed at which your relationship is progressing, the two of you are on your way straight to the altar."

"Oh! Lizzy! Please do not say that."

"Whyever not? How else does one explain his mother inviting you to the theater this evening as her guest?"

"I must say it was very generous of her to do so."

"It cannot hurt to have the mother's blessing so early in one's courtship."

Thoughts of Mr. Darcy's proposal could not help but intrude. Elizabeth could never imagine Mr. Hemmingsworth professing his love for Jane in such an ungentlemanly manner. *Jane's new beau will never subject her to such a speech.*

"I saw Mr. Bingley at the theater," Jane said, her voice almost a nostalgic whisper.

"You did, Jane? Why did you not tell me?"

"I suppose it just slipped my mind until now, in part because there was not much to tell."

Elizabeth decided not to press. She had decided never to interfere in Jane's love life again. Till that moment, Elizabeth had said nothing of seeing Bingley's friend either. She could not help but consider the irony of Jane, after countless weeks of hoping for a reunion with the gentleman, coming face-to-face with him on the eve of her departure from London.

"I was unlucky enough to spend time in company with his sisters, Mrs. Hurst and Miss Bingley," Elizabeth said. In an effort to be completely forthcoming, she added, "As well as Mr. Bingley's friend Mr. Darcy."

"Where was Mr. Hemmingsworth during the auspicious occasion?"

"He joined me," Elizabeth said. *Or rather rescued me,* she silently considered. "At which point I introduced him to the others."

"Including Mr. Darcy?"

"Yes—including Mr. Darcy. I do not see how I could have avoided it or why I would have, for that matter. Why do you ask?"

"I always suspected Mr. Darcy harbored a tender regard for you, I suppose. Not that I would ever expect him to act on it."

If only you knew, Elizabeth considered. Sidestepping the topic of Mr. Darcy, she asked, "And what of Mr. Bingley? Did you introduce him to your Mr. Hemmingsworth?"

"Yes—I did introduce the gentlemen. As you said, I do not see how I could have avoided it—or why I would have for that matter."

"Well, Jane, do not keep me in suspense. Pray, what was Mr. Bingley's reaction to seeing you again after all this time?"

"Surprised. I suspect he wanted to do more than exchange cordial civilities. Thankfully, Mr. Hemmingsworth remained a faithful companion, and I did not need to face Mr. Bingley alone."

"But if you suspected his need to talk, surely it is only a matter of time before the two of you do so."

Jane sighed. "I suppose that is true—but not tonight." She leaned toward the bedside table and blew out the candle. "If we are to set off for Hertfordshire as early as planned, we had better get some sleep."

With so much to consider and even more to conceal, Elizabeth knew it would be a while before she succumbed to slumber.

You must allow me to tell you how ardently I admire and love you.

No doubt these words would linger in her mind and never more than in that moment after having been reunited, if only for a short time, with the only man in the world who had ever uttered them to her.

Mr. Darcy.

CHAPTER 6

EXERCISE IN FUTILITY

HERTFORDSHIRE, ENGLAND - LONGBOURN VILLAGE

Longbourn's busy matriarch, Mrs. Fanny Bennet, burst into the dining room. All the family sat around the breakfast table—Mr. Thomas Bennet, the sharp-witted patriarch, the two eldest daughters recently returned from town, Jane and Elizabeth, and the remaining three girls in descending order of age—Mary, Kitty, and Lydia. A rich assortment of meats, cheeses, slices of bread, and fruit stretched before their eyes. Two female servants stood silently by the paneled wall, eager to be of help.

"Mr. Bennet," cried his lady, taking her usual seat,

"have you heard the news?"

"What news is that?" he replied, his eyes poring over his paper.

"Why, it is Grandover Park. It is recently bought—at last!"

Still eyeing his paper with intent, the gentleman scoffed. "Déjà vu."

A woman of mean understanding, little information, and uncertain temper, Mrs. Bennet said, "This is no time for you to be speaking your secret language that nobody understands. Surely you must realize what this means for our girls."

Lowering his paper, Mr. Bennet directed his attention to his wife. "I suppose you are going to tell me Grandover is taken by a single young man of large fortune from one or another part of England and he was so much delighted with it he agreed to take the place at once. Furthermore, you mean for him to marry one of our daughters. As that is no doubt his design in coming here, the only question I can think of is what is his name?"

"Hemmingsworth. What is more, he is said to have seven or eight thousand pounds a year."

"Hemmingsworth, you say?" Mr. Bennet rubbed his silver beard. "Which of our five daughters is to be his lucky bride?"

"Why, whichever one he chooses to fall in love with—so long as his choice is not Lizzy. We all know what a waste of time that would be on the gentleman's part."

Elizabeth, who theretofore attended her parents' conversation with amusement, took umbrage at such a remark. "Mamma!" she exclaimed in her own defense.

Knowing what she did, Elizabeth stole a glance at Jane, who quietly sipped her hot tea, paying no heed to her mother. To that day, the elder sister had remained silent on the subject of the Hemmingsworths with everyone in the room except Elizabeth.

Mrs. Bennet picked up a piece of bread and smeared it with strawberry jam. "What did I say that is untrue?" She shrugged. "Anyone who would refuse the hand of the heir of her family's estate cannot be trusted to do the right thing. Mr. Hemmingsworth had much better fall in love with Jane or even my Lydia."

Jane picked up her linen napkin and dabbed her lips. She slid her chair back from the table. "I think I should like to be excused."

"I shall join you," said Elizabeth, standing. She and Jane headed for the door.

"The two of you barely touched your plates," said Mrs. Bennet. "You must eat more—especially you, Jane. You will want to be in excellent health when you meet Mr. Hemmingsworth, my child." She eyed her husband. "Mr. Bennet! Say something."

What an exercise in futility, for Mr. Bennet could never bother himself to do his wife's bidding when it came to such matters. Whereas the business of Mrs. Bennet's life was marrying off her five daughters, the business of her husband's life, it seemed, was to let his children fend for themselves.

The two sisters kept walking, giving their eager mother no mind. When they were alone, Elizabeth said, "Dearest Jane, it appears you are quite intent on keeping your acquaintance with Mr. Hemmingsworth a secret."

"Can you blame me? Speaking of déjà vu, the last thing I want is a repeat of the Netherfield fiasco."

No, Elizabeth could not blame Jane for her stance. Nor could she deny the similarity to the arrival of another single man of large fortune in Hertfordshire in under a year. Mr. Charles Bingley. She would never forget the fuss her mother made at the time. Who was to say how Jane's relationship with Mr. Bingley might have progressed if not for her mother's shenanigans?

Heaven forbid Jane's budding relationship with Mr. Hemmingsworth should be upended before it has a fair chance to take root.

Just as Charles Bingley had inherited a fortune from his father, its origins rooted in trade, so had Mr. Hemmingsworth. Like the late Mr. Bingley, the late Mr. Hemmingsworth always meant to purchase an estate but did not live to do it. Unlike Charles Bingley, who merely let Netherfield Park, Stanford Hemmingsworth had bought the Grandover Park estate. Not that the latter was impulsive in his decision to do so. Indeed, relying upon Mr. Gardiner's counsel, Hemmingsworth made a sound purchase. He meant to make Hertfordshire his home.

Part of Elizabeth's active mind wished he had done it for Jane. She could not help wondering if Jane felt the same. "No doubt all such efforts to maintain secrecy will be in vain the moment the two of you are reunited. How shall you explain your undeniable attachment?" asked Elizabeth.

"I see no reason for us to worry about any of that now. Let us wait until Mr. Hemmingsworth and I meet again, and then I shall know how to feel."

Elizabeth knew it was not as simple as Jane was making it out to be. Indeed, the knowledge of an existing acquaintance with the Hemmingsworths was not the only thing being withheld from Mrs. Bennet. There was also the matter of two gentlemen with whom Mrs. Bennet was thoroughly acquainted calling on the Bennet daughters at Cheapside on the same day of their recent departure from town.

Mrs. Gardiner wrote some days ago informing Jane that Mr. Bingley had called on her along with his friend Mr. Darcy. Jane was determined to keep this news away from her mother.

She had lost count of the number of times she had written to her mother during her stay in town in response to the latter's persistent inquiry about the gentleman. So far as Jane was concerned, her mother, by now, had completely abandoned the idea of Jane being the future mistress of Netherfield.

Jane preferred to keep it that way, even if, by her own admission to Elizabeth, Bingley's visit awakened her curiosity about his purpose for calling on her after so many months had passed, especially when he could not find time for her when she was in town.

Of course, Jane shared the news with Elizabeth. It was not as though the two sisters had not speculated on such a possibility. Elizabeth's sentiments on hearing that Mr. Darcy had gone with his friend were a mixture of wonder and supposition.

No doubt he had acted merely in service to his friend was the explanation Elizabeth offered Jane. However, the story she told herself was not nearly as simple as that. Mr. Darcy in Cheapside! Mr. Darcy willingly throwing himself in the path of people whom he had derided as being beneath him in consequence. What was more, Mr. Darcy willingly throwing himself in her way?

Perhaps this is his way of letting me know he does not harbor any ill will toward me for the harsh mode of my rejection, Elizabeth could not help but consider.

Part of her wished she and Jane had not left town when they did.

To have seen firsthand how Mr. Darcy comported himself among my London relatives would have been something.

If nothing else, she would have suffered the satisfaction of seeing the look on his face upon realizing that she had fashionable relations of sense and education and of whom she was just as proud as he was of his noble family.

The whole business of Mr. Darcy's purposes for venturing to Cheapside, of all places, really gave Elizabeth something to think of.

Perchance, she would have seen in his eyes a measure of regret in having proposed to her in such an ungentlemanly manner.

Perchance, I would have seen a man with some willingness to atone, not only for his offenses against my sister but also for his officiousness toward me.

CHAPTER 7

A SECRET ADMIRER

*E*very available servant at Longbourn paraded into the drawing room bearing large, colorful bouquets of flowers. The housekeeper, Mrs. Hill, oversaw the floral placements throughout the room. It was the morning after an assembly in Meryton.

"What exquisite flowers!" Mrs. Bennet proclaimed. "And such lovely colors. The sender must have purchased every available blossom between here and London," she said as she pored over them. "Pray, do you have any indication of who the sender is?" she asked, directing her inquiry to Mrs. Hill.

"No, Madam. I was told the sender asked to be kept anonymous. I dared not press."

Mrs. Bennet waltzed across the room, seized her

eldest daughter's arm, and steered her toward one of the arrangements. "Dearest Jane, how fortunate you are. I always said you could not be so beautiful for nothing," she said, her voice teeming with satisfaction and pride. "All our friends will surely envy you now!"

"I would not be so quick to assume the flowers are for Jane, my dear," said Mr. Bennet, peering over his paper. "What of our four other daughters? Especially my Lizzy. No doubt, she was not without her own fair share of admirers at last night's assembly."

"Lizzy? Oh, Mr. Bennet, how you love to vex me. Why in the world would anyone send flowers to such an obstinate, headstrong girl as Lizzy? Why on earth must you always be giving her such preference?"

"Perhaps being obstinate and headstrong is the fashion," said Mr. Bennet. His eyes twinkled with a hint of merriment and mischief. "By my count, Lizzy is the only one of our fair daughters to have received an offer of marriage."

Lowering her eyes, Elizabeth placed a gentle hand on her elder sister's arm. Jane, of all people, did not deserve such a slight, even if it was unintentionally applicable to her situation.

Her mother scoffed. "And look at what became of that. Charlotte Lucas now stands in line to be the next mistress of this home because of it. Mr. Collins would have been far wiser had he offered for Jane instead—or even Mary, who I am sure would have been happy to have him."

As much as Elizabeth revered her father, she did not like being the means of his frustrating her mother. Wanting to put an end to the discussion, she said, "Well, regardless of who sent the flowers to whom, they are lovely indeed. There is no reason any of the five of us cannot pretend a secret admirer of our very own sent them."

"What nonsense, Lizzy! Jane's secret admirer and Jane's alone sent the flowers. The only question I have is which of her two beaus is the one—Mr. Hemmingsworth or Mr. Bingley."

Mr. Bennet peered over the rim of his glasses. "Mr. Bingley, you say? Now that is a name I have not heard mentioned for a while."

"Yes!" Mrs. Bennet cried. "Mr. Bingley has returned to Netherfield Park—a little late by my calculation." She shrugged. "Better late than never, I suppose."

Young Kitty scoffed. "Too late, by my calculation, for our dearest Jane has caught the eye of the handsome Mr. Hemmingsworth. I daresay Mr. Bingley does not stand a chance of winning her back."

"Kitty!" Jane cried in an attempt to rein in her sister's exuberance.

"I do not think I have seen a more handsome gentleman who cannot boast of being an officer," said Lydia. "The same goes for his brother, of course."

"How fortunate that you all have met the newest two eligible men to grace our society—with no trouble at all on my part, I might add. How fortunate indeed," said Mr. Bennet, returning his eyes to his paper.

"No trouble at all on your part, indeed. What a shame having been bested by the Lucases once again. Sir William took such delight in making the introductions. Not that it mattered, for once the elder brother was introduced to my Jane, he only had eyes for her."

"It would seem our Jane was the brightest jewel at the ball," said Mr. Bennet. He glanced at Elizabeth. "And what of you, my Lizzy? Were you as fortunate as your sister?"

Before Elizabeth could reply, Lydia said, "La! Poor Lizzy had the misfortune of dancing with the proud Mr. Darcy—Mr. Bingley's friend. No one could envy her, I am sure."

Mrs. Bennet nodded her head in agreement. "No one—not even your Lizzy could compare to Jane."

"Oh! What a delightful inconvenience indeed to have two handsome beaus from which to choose," said Kitty.

"I daresay I agree," Mrs. Bennet uttered, "however,

if forced to choose between Jane's beaus, I would have to favor Mr. Hemmingsworth, for sure."

"And why is that, my dear?" asked Mr. Bennet.

"Did you not hear Lydia mention before that Mr. Hemmingsworth has a brother who is just as handsome as he is? Indeed, they are twins! Why! He would be perfect for one of our other girls. Jane's marrying the elder of the two must surely bode well for one of her sisters." She clasped her hands. "Oh, I do hope the two gentlemen will call on Longbourn today as I will be sure to invite them to take a family dinner."

"I am afraid you will surely have to wait, for I heard Mrs. Long telling Mrs. Greene the gentlemen were to return to London today," said Mary. Likely overcome by the fragrance of so many fresh-cut flowers, she sneezed.

"Already?" Mrs. Bennet cried, spinning on her heel to regard her middle child directly. "For heaven's sake, they have hardly settled, and they are traipsing off to town already! I do hope it is not a sign of their being fickle. We have suffered through enough of that with our Netherfield neighbor."

Knowing this quip was a reference to Mr. Bingley, Elizabeth suffered some discomfort for her elder sister. In espousing her frustration with the young man's capricious behavior, her mother had unwittingly slighted Jane. One look at Jane confirmed this notion. Jane, who rarely revealed her true feelings to anyone, stared out the window, her countenance disheartened.

Mary said, "In the Hemmingsworths' case, there is a perfect reason for their journey. I heard they have gone to town for the sole purpose of bringing their mother to Hertfordshire upon their return." She grabbed her dainty white handkerchief and held it to her nose. "Achoo!"

CHAPTER 8

ONE NOTICEABLE EXCEPTION

While on their way to Longbourn to call on the eldest Bennet daughters, Mr. Bingley and Mr. Darcy espied the two sisters walking arm in arm on the lane just up ahead. Surely this was their lucky day. There was no sign of the two gentlemen whom both Bingley and Darcy marked as rivals after competing against them for their share of Jane's and Elizabeth's affections, respectively, at the Meryton assembly.

Bingley had learned of the assembly in Meryton that very evening on the heels of his return to Netherfield along with his friend. Consequently, the gentlemen's arrival at the lively gathering caught everyone by surprise. Waves of whispers circulating throughout the crowded room attested to everyone's shock.

Almost every eye in the room fell on Miss Bennet. Hushed whispers questioned Bingley's being there after his hasty departure last November. The answers grew evident as the young man made his way directly to his previously abandoned lover's side.

Bingley was no stranger to such unabashed displays of affection and admiration. He rarely strayed from Jane's side from that moment on, even if the newcomer, Stanford Hemmingsworth, steadfastly comported himself likewise.

Mr. Darcy, on the other hand, was not accustomed to expressing his admiration in so blatant a fashion. Rather than plant himself by Elizabeth and her new admirer's sides, he chose to keep moving about the room. He rarely stayed in one spot long enough to indulge in conversation with anyone. In essentials, he was very much the same man who had attended the Meryton assembly the year before.

There was one noticeable exception, however. Mr. Darcy made sure to dance with Elizabeth and only Elizabeth that evening. And not just one set but two. In that respect, it mattered not what people thought. He would not let it be said that this new fellow from town—one half of a pair of eligible young men— commanded the bulk of Elizabeth's attention.

The gentlemen from Netherfield Park immediately

leaped from their horses to their feet and approached the Bennet sisters.

Bingley, whose countenance bespoke all his pleasure, said, "Miss Bennet, Miss Elizabeth." He bowed slightly and continued, "This is indeed a pleasant surprise. Darcy and I were just on our way to Longbourn to call on you." He turned to his friend. "Were we not, Darcy?"

The other man nodded. "Indeed." He too bowed before the young ladies.

Jane and Elizabeth both curtsied in their turn. Smiling, Jane said, "Good morning, sirs. It is such a fine morning. My sister and I are on our way to Oakham Mount. You are welcome to join us." Here, she turned to her younger sister. "Are they not, Lizzy?"

"I am sure you are most welcome, sirs. But what of your horses?" Elizabeth asked, eyeing the two giant beasts circumspectly.

Darcy said, "Are you not fond of horses, Miss Elizabeth?"

"As you know, sir, I much prefer walking—"

"Yes, I know," he said, nodding.

"Of course, you can have no idea of my reason."

"I am afraid there are a great many things I do not know about you, Miss Elizabeth. Perhaps we can take this time to correct that—starting with your love of walking. Tell me anything except you fear horses."

"I fear you are correct, sir. Horses are among my least favorite creatures in the world." Her spirits rising to playfulness, she said, "Now, hate me if you dare."

"I think you know that hate is not a word that might ever be used to describe my feelings for you, Miss Elizabeth."

Despite the brevity of their intercourse, the two had failed in noticing Jane and Bingley had already proceeded walking toward Oakham Mount.

In that same vein as her earlier retort, Elizabeth said, "No—but surely you must pity me. An impertinent country lass who is afraid of horses."

The playfulness in her voice lifted Darcy's spirits considerably and encouraged him to respond in a similar fashion.

"Whatever am I to do with you?" he asked. Seizing this chance to improve her opinion of him, he added, "What would you say if I offered to teach you to ride? Surely that would go a long way toward easing your discomfort."

"I suppose it could not hurt. Saying that, I would hate to impose upon you, sir. Who is to say how long such an endeavor would take? Surely you must be eager to return to town."

"Not particularly, Miss Elizabeth. I am happy to remain here in Hertfordshire for as long as it takes."

"May I have time to consider your offer, sir?"

"Indeed, take all the time you need. I am not going anywhere—except Oakham Mount, that is. Shall we be on our way?"

"And what of your horse?"

"I will allow him a longer rein than normal. Your comfort is my primary concern."

With that said, Darcy and Elizabeth commenced walking with his horse trailing far behind.

"I trust you enjoyed the flowers," said Mr. Darcy, having walked for some distance in companionable silence beside the woman who owned his heart.

"So, you are the mystery gentleman who sent all those lovely bouquets to Longbourn."

"Not to Longbourn, Miss Elizabeth. In sending the flowers, I believe I thought only of you."

A warm feeling washed all over her. "Thank you for your consideration, sir. I am honored. As much as I appreciate your secrecy, I am too curious not to ask what your reason was for shielding your identity."

"I did not think you would appreciate such a public display of my admiration for you. I presume you have told no one, save your elder sister perhaps, of what unfolded between us in Kent."

"Actually, sir, I have yet to confide the events that unfolded between us even to Jane."

Mr. Darcy's shoulders slumped. His dark, brooding eyes were cast downward.

Seeing this, Elizabeth said, "My reasoning has nothing to do with what you must be thinking, sir."

He threw her an inquisitive stare, which was encouragement enough for her to continue.

"I could not very well confide in her what happened without addressing the matter of Mr. Bingley's defection and the impetus behind it. Thus, I thought it best to say nothing on the subject at all."

"When I think back to the cold-hearted manner of my proposal to you, Miss Elizabeth, I am absolutely appalled with myself. I cannot very well blame you if you harbor some lingering ill will toward me because of it. I feel I did myself no service by the manner of my opening declaration in the letter I wrote.

He recalled his exact words: *"Be not alarmed, madam, on receiving this letter, by the apprehension of its containing any repetition of those sentiments or renewal of those offers that were last night so disgusting to you. I write without any intention of paining you or humbling myself by dwelling on wishes that, for the happiness of both, cannot be too soon forgotten—"*

"I deeply regret espousing such sentiments to you.

It took your painstaking rejection and a month of self-imposed exile for me to chart a different course in life. Upon returning to town and a subsequent talk with Bingley, I resolved to see you, hopefully to make amends and start anew.

"When I saw you mere hours later at the theater, I became more determined than ever to make amends for all the harm I had inflicted.

"I went to Cheapside the very next day to see you, but you and your sister had already left in return to Hertfordshire."

Mr. Darcy commenced a recital of all that he had intended to say to her that day. How despite failing to court her properly as he ought to have done, he had offered his hand to her, believing she shared the same feelings for him as he felt for her. He said if Elizabeth would but allow him the chance, this time he would comport himself as a man bent on winning his lady's heart ought to.

Concluding his speech, he said, "My love for you, though much too carefully concealed, has been long in the making. I now know that your feelings for me were more negative than favorable and understandably so. Instead of earning your good opinion, my every action served to turn you against me. I hope that is beginning to change."

With all of my objections to Mr. Darcy falling by the wayside, how can I possibly object to such a prospect?

Intending to give the gentleman every reason to suspect that her feelings had indeed changed, she extended her hand to him.

He seized it at once.

"I accept your offer, sir."

Mr. Darcy swallowed. His eyes opened wide.

Her spirits rising to playfulness, she asked, "When shall our riding lessons begin?"

Once Darcy and Elizabeth arrived at Oakham Mount, Jane and Bingley, who had been waiting for a while, joined them straightaway, forcing all subsequent conversation to resort to threadbare topics. For Elizabeth's part, this was just as well for Mr. Darcy had given her much to consider.

The avowal of his continued affection for her brought about a new understanding. A new beginning awaited them indeed—one set to commence with early morning, private horse riding lessons. Her reservations about learning that which she had managed to put off for years notwithstanding, Elizabeth could hardly wait for this chance to start anew with Mr. Fitzwilliam Darcy.

"Would you believe, Lizzy, that when Mr. Bingley went to town last November, he really loved me, and nothing but a persuasion of my being indifferent would have prevented his coming down again?" Jane said upon her return from Oakham Mount with her sister. They had parted with the two gentlemen from Netherfield without accepting Mr. Bingley's offer to accompany them all the way.

Having plucked several flowers from among the many floral arrangements in the drawing room to create her own bouquet for her bedroom, Elizabeth retrieved one from its vase, drew in its scent and slowly exhaled. Despite being somewhat conflicted by her sister's declaration, she smiled.

How could she not but feel that way? Not only had Mr. Darcy, her own *would-be* suitor, as of that very day been instrumental in persuading Bingley of Jane's supposed indifference, but he had confessed his part in the scheme to Elizabeth. She had kept it all from Jane. At first, Elizabeth had persuaded herself that she was merely protecting her sister from further suffering. As day after day passed by, Elizabeth could not say with certitude that she was not simply protecting Mr. Darcy.

Her *would-be* suitor. She reflected on this new depiction of the gentleman, for how else was Elizabeth to describe him? That a gentleman would propose to a woman who had rejected him once was incomprehensible—especially for a gentleman like Mr. Darcy.

Another supposed suitor whom she had rejected came to mind—Mr. Collins, particularly his response: *"You must give me leave to flatter myself, my dear cousin, that your refusal of my addresses is merely words, of course."*

The ridiculous man had even threatened that, despite Elizabeth's various attractions, it was by no means certain that another offer of marriage may ever be made to her.

Concluding his rebuttal, he had declared, *"Your portion is unhappily so small that it will in all likelihood undo the effects of your loveliness and amiable qualifications. As I must therefore conclude that you are not serious in your rejection of me, I shall choose to attribute it to your wish of increasing my love by suspense, according to the usual practice of elegant females."*

And yet, Mr. Darcy had declared his intention to court her properly. Where else would the successful pursuit of such a courtship end but at the wedding altar?

"Lizzy? Did you not hear what I just said?" Jane asked, interrupting her sister's silent reverie.

Elizabeth nodded. "I always suspected as much,

dearest Jane. Mr. Bingley would have to have been a fool not to fall in love with you."

"I know you always had faith in his love for me, even when my heart had its fair share of doubt."

"Pray, does this mean you have forgiven him and you are ready to resume where you two left off in November?"

"You know as well as I do that it is not as simple as that."

"I take it you are speaking of your budding romance with Mr. Hemmingsworth."

"I do not know that it is fair to characterize our acquaintance as a budding romance."

"Then how would you describe it?"

"Oh, Lizzy! The time I have spent getting acquainted with Mr. Hemmingsworth ranks among the happiest times in my life. When we are together, I never wish to be parted from him. When we are apart, it is all I can do not to think of him."

"Are you saying you are already in love with Mr. Hemmingsworth?"

"I—I hardly know how to describe my feelings for him, especially since I was sure that I was in love with Mr. Bingley for so many months before making Mr. Hemmingsworth's acquaintance."

"Does that mean you are still in love with Mr. Bingley?"

Jane shrugged. "That I cannot say with certitude. I know I no longer suffer the pain of our abrupt separation as sorely as I once did. Do I not owe it to him to give him another chance?"

Elizabeth shook her head. "No—you do not owe Mr. Bingley anything. The only thing that matters is your obligation to yourself. If you fear you will forever suffer regret in not allowing Mr. Bingley to make amends, then you must decide based on that."

Jane sighed. "If I am to be honest, I would have to say that I do not want to injure either of the gentlemen. As selfish as that sounds, it is truly how I feel."

"Well, Jane, there is no law that forbids you from enjoying the attentions of both Mr. Bingley and Mr. Hemmingsworth, is there?"

"I am certain my mother would not wish for me to behave in such a manner—not when she is so eager to get rid of all of us."

"Jane, you are so good. While I am certain I shall never be as good as you, perhaps in such a case as this you should follow my example."

"What do you mean, Lizzy?"

"I posit you must pay no attention to our mother, especially where your own felicity is concerned. She would have happily seen me married to Mr. Collins after all." Elizabeth seized her sister's hand. "If my rejection of my cousin's hand is not license for you to act in accordance with your own wishes, I do not know what is."

CHAPTER 9

HER HEART OF HEARTS

Unbeknownst to Mrs. Bennet, Mr. Bennet had called on the Hemmingsworths soon after they arrived in Hertfordshire, mere days before the Meryton assembly. What was more, he had known of Mr. Stanford Hemmingsworth's plans to buy the Grandover Park estate before it was settled upon, owing to regular correspondence with his brother-in-law Mr. Edward Gardiner.

Mr. Bennet was not one to confide such intelligence in his wife, for where was the fun in that? Far better that he appeared indifferent and watched events unfold. Making sport of the ridiculousness of others was the business of his life. Nothing amused him more than watching his wife go about the business of her life—that being marrying off her five daughters. Had his wife had her way, his favorite daughter would be living far away in Kent with the nonsensical Mr. Collins. Mr. Bennet, in siding with Elizabeth, had put an end to such foolishness.

On the other hand, the favorite wish of his wife to see their first-born daughter married to Mr. Charles Bingley was one that he would have supported wholeheartedly. But, alas, the hoped-for proposal never came about. Mr. Bennet suspected his wife's foolishness had a part to play in the unfortunate outcome. He never meant to be a party to his wife's matchmaking schemes—even unconsciously—hence he kept everything he knew about the Hemmingsworths to himself —everything.

Despite Mr. Bingley's return, all the Bennets' neighbors and acquaintances whispered of an alliance between Jane and Stanford Hemmingsworth. Similarly, they speculated on a possible alliance between Elizabeth and Mitchell Hemmingsworth. Mrs. Bennet was a happy woman indeed.

The lady was overcome with joy when the Hemmingsworth brothers called on Longbourn, almost on the heels of their return from town. Mr. Bennet contented himself with the usual civilities. He then escaped to the comforts of his library, leaving his wife to the business of what she did best.

"I trust you settled your business in town without too much trouble," said Mrs. Bennet to one of the new guests.

Though identical in countenance and in comportment, the gentlemen bore a telling distinction by the manner in which they wore their hair. The younger twin sported a slightly curlier mane. One needing another means of distinguishing the two brothers had only to see the way the first-born looked at Jane whenever they were in company.

In response to Mrs. Bennet's inquiry, the older brother replied that he had indeed handled his affairs in town.

"And what of your mother? I was given to believe she would return to Grandover Park with you."

"A prior commitment prevented her from returning with us, I am afraid. However, my mother is looking forward to meeting all of you. Therefore, I would like to take this opportunity to invite your family to dine at Grandover once she arrives and things are better settled."

Mrs. Bennet raised her hand to her bosom. "Why! I am sure we shall be delighted," she began, "and by all means, the two of you are welcome to dine here at Longbourn as often as your plans will allow. We are most honored by your presence."

"It is an honor to be so well received by all your family," replied the elder brother, looking at Jane.

Mrs. Bennet bestowed a look of utter approbation on her guest. "My Jane is equally honored, I am sure."

"Well, that being the case, my happiness is complete," said Stanford Hemmingsworth.

"Indeed. My Jane is sure to make one lucky gentleman the happiest man in the world. She and all my daughters are brought up very properly. All our friends and acquaintances highly regard them—Jane in particular.

"My neighbor, Lady Lucas herself, has often said so and envied me Jane's beauty. I do not like to boast of my own child, but to be sure, one rarely sees anybody better looking than Jane. It is what everybody says. I do not trust my own partiality. When she was only fifteen, there was a man at my brother Gardiner's in town so much in love with her that my sister-in-law was sure he would make her an offer before we came away. However, he did not. Perhaps he thought her too young. However, he wrote some pretty verses on her. They were charming indeed," Mrs. Bennet concluded, nodding her head.

Having heard this assertion spoken almost verbatim to Charles Bingley last year at Netherfield, Elizabeth was sure she did not wish to have her mother carry on in such an unabashed manner with yet another suitor—even if Mr. Hemmingsworth looked as though he hardly paid Mrs. Bennet any mind. Instead, his attention was fixed on Jane.

"What better efficacy in driving away love than a poem," said Elizabeth.

"I would imagine it depends on the skill of its delivery, Miss Elizabeth," said the younger brother.

This reply did not surprise her. Mitchell Hemmingsworth took such pleasure in challenging her.

"That is exactly what I expected you to say," Elizabeth replied.

"No doubt because you know me so well," said he.

"That you choose to argue a perfectly valid point merely for the sake of being contrary—"

"Lizzy, pray, remember yourself," Mrs. Bennet cried, interrupting her daughter's speech. "Sir, I hope you will forgive our Lizzy. At times, she cannot help but say whatever is on her mind. But I assure you within her heart of hearts, she knows a woman's place."

While Elizabeth and Mitchell exchanged mocking, surreptitious glances, Mrs. Bennet embarked upon a lengthy recital with the design of assuring the elder brother of all Jane's estimable qualities. Indeed, any man would be lucky to have her.

The younger two girls had been whispering to each other and nudging each other throughout the visit. When, finally, a lull in the conversation presented itself, Lydia said, "What say you to the idea of giving a ball, Mr. Hemmingsworth?"

Kitty clasped her hands in front of her smiling face. "Pray, give a ball!"

Jane looked at Elizabeth. Elizabeth looked at Jane. The latter lowered her eyes.

"Lydia! Kitty! Pray do not dare importune on our guest this way," Elizabeth implored on her older sister's behalf.

"Why in heavens not?" Lydia asked. "The gentlemen are new to our society, and they have yet to meet so many of their new neighbors. What better way to form new acquaintances than at a ball?"

Elizabeth's heart ached for her elder sister, who had yet to raise her head. Jane's suitor must have noticed her unease too.

"It is true I have yet to meet many of my new neighbors," he said. He turned to gaze at Jane. "On the other hand, I believe I am very well acquainted with the one who matters most."

Understanding the gentleman was speaking of

herself, Jane's eyes met his. Seeing this, Elizabeth could not have been more pleased. She silently prayed that would be the end of the conversation—albeit in vain.

"Mr. Bingley gave a ball at Netherfield last November!" Lydia exclaimed with the liveliness one might expect of someone so young, whose primary enjoyment was flirting and dancing.

Jane colored. Elizabeth felt her own color rising as well, partly because of her remembrance of what had happened in the immediate aftermath of the Netherfield ball. Mr. Bingley's leave-taking pained her still.

Mr. Hemmingsworth said, "Fear not, Miss Lydia, for I plan to remain in Hertfordshire for an exceedingly long time. No doubt, I shall give many balls at Grandover Park over the coming years."

The younger girls burst into silly peals of laughter and hugged each other, undoubtedly pleased with this reply. Elizabeth exhaled—not that her sisters' making a spectacle of themselves was cause for relief but because they had averted the topic of the Netherfield ball.

She gazed outside a nearby window. The sun shone brightly, and the swaying of the tree leaves hinted at a gentle breeze. The flowers dotting the landscape had burst with colors of late spring. Her mind drifted three miles away to the neighboring estate—Netherfield Park. Memories of having danced with Mr. Darcy last November gave way to memories of having spent time alone with him that very morning horse riding on the outskirts of the estate. *How different he is now than the man whom I thought him to be then.*

Her mother's voice pierced Elizabeth's silent musing.

"I suspect Mr. Hemmingsworth has never seen the view from Oakham Mount," said Mrs. Bennet. "It is such a lovely day for a walk. Perchance, Jane and Lizzy, the two of you might venture there with our guests. It is such a long walk—a delightful walk, to be sure. I dare not ask any of the other girls to join you. None of them are particularly good walkers," she added, directing the last part to the guests.

After nearly an hour watching her mother's none too subtle matchmaking machinations, this was an offer neither Elizabeth nor Jane dared to refuse, and soon the four young people were on their way.

CHAPTER 10

A WAY WITH WORDS

Minutes after the foursome took their leave, Mrs. Hill walked into the room. "Mr. Darcy and Mr. Bingley," she said. The two gentlemen stood side-by-side upon entering the room—one anxious, the other cool and reserved.

"Mr. Bingley!" exclaimed Mrs. Bennet. "Why, this is a surprise indeed." She threw a glance at his friend. "Mr. Darcy, your presence is no less of a surprise, I am sure."

Mr. Darcy merely nodded.

"It is a long time, Mr. Bingley, since you went away," said Mrs. Bennet after the guests had taken their seats.

He readily agreed to it.

"I was afraid you would never come back again. So

many changes have happened in the neighborhood since you went away. Miss King has gone away to Liverpool after having inherited ten thousand pounds.

"The militia has left for Brighton and has thus deprived us of the colorful Lieutenant Wickham—what a perfect gentleman. Oh! And Miss Lucas is married and settled. I suppose you have heard of it. Indeed, you must have seen it in the papers."

Bingley replied that he had.

"Indeed, Miss Lucas married our own Mr. Collins," Mrs. Bennet said. "It is a shame to be sure, for she and Mr. Collins may turn my poor daughters and me out as soon as they please, once Mr. Bennet is dead. But, alas, some daughters are wiser than others where honoring one's familial responsibility is concerned."

Bingley hardly paid attention to Mrs. Bennet at all. He was far too busy looking at the doorway—that or staring out the windows. And, at length, the young man's anxious state drew Kitty's notice.

"Are you looking for someone, Mr. Bingley?"

"La!" Lydia cried. "You know very well he is looking for our Jane."

"I am afraid you have missed her," said Mrs. Bennet. "You see, Jane and Lizzy left not fifteen minutes ago."

"Left?" Mr. Darcy asked, drawing everyone's attention by his abruptness. Then, after an awkward pause, he continued, "Have they returned to town?"

"They walked with the Hemmingsworths to Oakham Mount," said Mary.

"I suppose if you hurry, you might catch them," said Kitty.

"What nonsense," her mother cried, taking umbrage at her daughter's suggestion. It was not as though Mrs. Bennet was displeased to see Mr. Bingley, but she did not want to risk him getting in Mr. Hemmingsworth's way.

Between Mr. Bingley and Mr. Hemmingsworth, the latter held a decided advantage where Mrs. Bennet's ever-constant matchmaking schemes were concerned. Not only was he wealthier, but he had never been the means of disappointing her family's hopes. Mr. Bingley, on the other hand, needed to prove himself once again worthy of Mrs. Bennet's unabashed approbation.

"Why I am sure neither of the gentlemen knows the way," she said.

"On the contrary," Mr. Bingley said, shaking his head, "I have gone there on several occasions, even as recently as yesterday."

"Then surely you have grown tired of seeing the view by now. I am sure nothing has changed."

"I think I will take Miss Kitty up on her suggestion, nevertheless. What say you, Darcy?"

"I have found time spent seeing the view from Oakham Mount quite agreeable. It would be a shame to forgo the possibility of an equally pleasurable diversion today."

"Then it is decided." Both gentlemen arose from their seats, made quick work of bidding the four Longbourn women adieu, and took their leave.

Darcy and Bingley were well on their way to Oakham Mount when they espied the Bennet sisters and the Hemmingsworth brothers heading back to Longbourn. They dared not pretend the aim of their sojourn had nothing to do with spending time in company with Jane and Elizabeth. Hence, they turned and walked with them once they were all face-to-face and had dispensed with all the usual civilities.

Before long, Jane and her beaus had outpaced Elizabeth and hers. The latter three of them walked in companionable silence, the gentlemen at either of Elizabeth's sides. She could only imagine what the two men were thinking.

She was on the verge of speaking when Mitchell

Hemmingsworth cleared his throat.

"Although this is a lovely day for a walk, I wager horse riding would be just as refreshing," said the younger man. "What say you, Miss Elizabeth?"

Before she could fashion a reply, Mr. Darcy said, "Miss Elizabeth is particularly fond of walking."

"No doubt," Hemmingsworth said. "Who does not enjoy a brisk walk now and then? Surely this does not negate one's desire for a speedier mode of moving about. Do you agree, Miss Elizabeth?"

"I dare not argue your point, sir. Suffice it to say, not everyone is in the position of enjoying such a pursuit. I, for one, have an aversion where horse riding is concerned."

"Surely you are not afraid of horses, Miss Elizabeth!"

"You might say that," she said.

"Then you must allow me to help you overcome said objections," said Mr. Hemmingsworth.

"Miss Elizabeth already has someone to assist her in overcoming her reservations," Mr. Darcy said.

The younger man looked at Elizabeth questioningly. "Oh?"

Elizabeth said, "Mr. Darcy offered to teach me to ride horseback as a means of overcoming my fear, and I have accepted his proposal—"

Then, catching herself, she said, "I mean to say his offer—I accepted his offer."

"Is that so?" Hemmingsworth asked, his brow arched.

Hardly knowing how to look or feel after such a telling blunder, Elizabeth half-smiled.

"Surely one can benefit from expertise from multiple sources. Hence my offer stands," Hemmingsworth countered.

"Once I am done with the lessons I have in mind for Miss Elizabeth, I doubt she will wish to pursue them with another," said Mr. Darcy.

"I must say, Mr. Darcy, you certainly do have a way with words. You seem to imply more than you state."

"Do I?"

"Perchance you pride yourself on possessing such a talent."

"Be careful what you say, Mr. Hemmingsworth. Take care you do not put words in my mouth that would not otherwise be there."

The other man gave him a look. "As I was speaking of whether Miss Elizabeth will avail herself of my offer, only time will tell."

"Is that so?"

"Indeed. Miss Elizabeth and I likely will spend a lot of time in each other's company now that my brother and I have settled here in Hertfordshire. We cannot always walk to Oakham Mount—despite its various enticements."

Inwardly, Elizabeth gulped. *Is Mr. Hemmingsworth deliberately trying to provoke Mr. Darcy?* she wondered. She glanced toward Mr. Darcy.

He turned to face her, his eyes brooding. Elizabeth did not know what to think. Was he angry or simply annoyed?

"Perchance your time with Miss Elizabeth in Hertfordshire will not last as long as you think."

"I do not see why I should not be able to be in company with Miss Elizabeth for years to come," Mr. Hemmingsworth said.

Mr. Darcy's response was instant. "Miss Elizabeth cannot always be of Longbourn."

Mr. Hemmingsworth did not blink. "True enough. We neither of us can predict what will happen in the future or where our paths will lead. Speaking of which, no doubt your path must surely soon lead you to Derbyshire. A man like you cannot always be away from your estate."

"I thank you for your concern about my comings and goings," Mr. Darcy said. "I assure you your concern is unwarranted. I always behave in my best interest. For the present as well as the indeterminate future, my current situation is the most advantageous arrangement for my purposes."

Meanwhile, in Kent, some mischief was afoot.

Mr. Collins, having read the missive he borrowed from Elizabeth without her knowing, had yet to find a way to use the information held therein to his advantage. What a conundrum he suffered, wanting to appease his noble patronage by imparting such vital knowledge as he possessed about her nephew's true intentions toward Miss Anne de Bourgh, or rather lack thereof. At the same time, he was withholding information that might damage his own standing in Lady Catherine's eyes, what with him knowing what he now knew about her noble family's brush with scandal.

Such information indeed would cause untold harm to the Fitzwilliam family were it made known.

The young man paced the floor with his hands clutched behind his back.

How would her ladyship want me to act in such a case as this? Collins wondered.

Weeks had passed since he last read Mr. Darcy's letter. He ought to have memorized every line, but he

SOMETHING TO THINK OF

had not. By now, he was not sure what he thought he knew.

He came to an abrupt halt. *First, I shall reread the letter, and then I shall have a better idea of how I ought to approach Lady Catherine.*

Collins hurried toward the door, eased it open, and poked his head just outside. He looked up and down the hallway. Then, seeing no one about, he listened for a few seconds more for good measure. The last thing he wanted was to be caught reading a letter he had no business with. How would he explain to Mrs. Collins how he came into possession of a letter from Mr. Darcy to her intimate friend?

Ducking his head back inside the room, he reached for the doorknob and turned the key, locking himself inside the room. Even this would not do. How would he explain a locked door in a household of two, the servants not counted? He could not—despite his dear wife's frequent habit of accidentally locking her bedroom door at night. Hence, Collins unlocked the door.

I shall simply tuck the letter inside a book. Then, should Mrs. Collins enter the room, she will be no more the wiser as to what I am reading.

After retrieving the perfect book to shield his covert purposes, he went to the secret place he had found behind his bureau to stash Mr. Darcy's letter. Old and worn, the back panel was covered in dust—thus an annoying hint to him to speak with the maid about this neglect.

Seconds later, stumbling backward, Collins clutched his chest. He could feel all the color drain from his face. The side of his body was resting against the side of the bureau; the next thing he knew, he slumped to the floor.

"Mr. Darcy's letter! It's—it's gone!" he croaked.

The next instant, the door flew wide open. Mrs. Collins stood inside the doorway; her eyes opened wide and trained on her husband. What was he doing cowering on the floor next to the bureau, his complexion a harrowing shade of pale?

"What on earth is the matter, Mr. Collins?" she asked, entering the room. "You look positively ill. You look almost as though you have seen a ghost!"

Deep inside, his lady did not know whether to laugh or to cry, for she knew exactly what was afoot and what her husband had done. Mr. Collins's anxious expression, the way he huddled close to the bureau—it was ridiculous. Ridiculous, abominable, and intolerable.

CHAPTER 11

KINDRED SPIRITS

The Hemmingsworth brothers took a family dinner with the Bennets at Longbourn that evening. For Mrs. Bennet's part, it was not as though she was showing a preference for one of Jane's suitors over the other. Had she not invited Charles Bingley to dine with her family many times theretofore? Circumstances, it seemed, always conspired against them. Even she knew the folly of too many beaus in the same place at one time. Nevertheless, there would be time enough to invite Mr. Bingley and, by default, his friend Mr. Darcy to a family dinner later in the week.

After dinner was served and everyone had gathered in the parlor for cards, Elizabeth found a minor distraction in the game. Ever since they parted in the lane, her mind had been busily engaged with thoughts of her earlier companion, Mr. Darcy. She especially thought of their plan to meet early the following day for her lesson. Even if she were an avid horsewoman, which, of course, Elizabeth was not, feigning ignorance was well worth the chance to be under Mr. Darcy's tutelage.

She could not help but wonder about the verbal sparring between Mr. Darcy and Mr. Hemmingsworth. The former bore it tolerably well, but Elizabeth would have much preferred a more civil stance between the two men. If only she could find a means of keeping the peace between them.

Glancing in Mitchell Hemmingsworth's direction, Elizabeth detected he was looking right at her, his eyes alight with merriment. The charming gentleman's welcoming smile was enough for her to forgive him for almost anything.

"Miss Elizabeth," Mr. Hemmingsworth said, "I see that you are very skilled at this game. Would you care to have a match of whist with me?"

"I would be delighted, sir," she said with a smile.

He and his chosen partner challenged her and hers to several games, which the latter won easily. As amused as she was, Elizabeth suspected he was letting them win. Everything she knew about him informed her that he was too competitive not to excel in whatever endeavor he set his mind to.

Upon first making his acquaintance in London, Elizabeth knew and understood it would be advantageous to her sister Jane's prospects if a friendship formed between Mr. Hemmingsworth and her. She never imagined she would enjoy his company as much as she did. Indeed, theirs was a genuine friendship—one of kindred spirits, Elizabeth liked to think.

If only he did not go out of his way to antagonize Mr. Darcy.

Later on, Mitchell Hemmingsworth, espying Elizabeth off to herself, approached her for a not unanticipated private tête-à-tête.

"Is there something you wish to tell me about your acquaintance with this Darcy fellow? Something I ought to know, perhaps?"

Having spent the better part of the afternoon with both gentlemen and detecting an abundance of none too subtle masculine showmanship between them, Mr. Hemmingsworth's question did not surprise Elizabeth. He was nothing if not direct. Direct and observant.

"I am sure there is nothing to tell," Elizabeth said slowly.

"May I ask you if there is a particular reason you are so attentive to the gentleman—and he to you?"

Elizabeth hesitated and considered Mr. Hemmingsworth's question for a moment. He had a good understanding of human nature. His observation was as genuine as could be, and she found it intriguing that they were so much alike in that regard.

However, Elizabeth had told no one about Mr. Darcy's marriage proposal—not even Jane. Surely this was not the time to reverse course. "Why do you ask such a question, Mr. Hemmingsworth?" she asked, handing him a cup of freshly poured hot coffee.

"Like you, I fancy myself an excellent studier of people's character. Based upon my observations of the two of you when in each other's company, I would say there is far more to your relationship than you would have anyone know. Pray, tell me if I am mistaken. One word from you will silence me on the subject."

"I cannot say that you are mistaken, sir. Or rather, I will not say you are not mistaken. The truth is I have spoken to no one other than Mr. Darcy himself on the matter. Therefore, I believe it to be a solemn trust, for lack of a better description, solely between the gentleman and me."

"I will not pry. I am sure you have your reasons for keeping secret affairs between you and the gentleman. Still, should you wish to confide in someone who is entirely impartial on the subject, I might add, I am more than willing to listen."

"Impartial, you say," Elizabeth began, her voice teasing and playful. "And what of our little ruse to protect you from all the matchmaking mammas in Meryton—including my own? The one that finds the two of us frequently enjoying each other's company?"

"Our little ruse indeed. I say that is all the more reason to take me into your confidence. How else shall we pass the time if not by regularly engaging in such stimulating intercourse?"

"Mr. Hemmingsworth!"

"What did I say?" he asked. Then, leaning a little closer, he said, "By the way, our little scheme is working, I think—at least where your mother is concerned. Not once has she hinted at an alliance between one of her daughters and me. Including you, I might add. Why is that?"

"I thought you wanted to be spared such attention on my mother's part. And yet you are questioning your good fortune."

"Do not willfully misunderstand me, Miss Elizabeth. I believe you know exactly what I meant. So why is your mother ignoring the possibility of an alliance between the two of us?"

"The reason is quite simple. You see, sir, my

mother has given up on the possibility of my ever marrying anyone. Therefore, were you to fall to your knees and request my hand in marriage this very moment, I am sure she would pay no attention at all."

The gentleman set his porcelain cup aside. "Shall we test your theory, Miss Elizabeth? I am willing if you are."

Elizabeth gasped. "You would not dare."

The gentleman laughed a little. "As tempting as you are, you are perfectly safe with me—for now. However, you have yet to answer my question to my satisfaction. Why has your mother given up on you? Surely her reasoning can have no factual basis. Your manifold attractions are too amazing to ignore."

She shrugged. "Were I to tell you, I fear your opinion of me might sour."

"Is it as dreadful as that?"

"My mother would say so, as would most of our neighbors and acquaintances, I am sure."

"And what does your father have to say?" he asked, once again standing straight and tall.

"Oh! He supported me, and in a manner my mother likely will not forget for as long as the three of us shall live."

"Now I am thoroughly intrigued. You must tell me all there is to tell."

"Well, sir, as we shall have ample opportunity for such intercourse, what say we defer this conversation until our circumstances allow us to do it justly?"

The young man leaned forward. "I plan to hold you to that, Miss Elizabeth," he said, his voice deep and rich, like fine intoxicating wine.

Elizabeth smiled. "I am sure you will." Then, inexplicably, an odd sensation that she could not immediately identify washed over her. Her smile froze in place, and her heart started pounding in her chest.

She was not afraid of Mitchell Hemmingsworth. However, she was beginning to suspect that were it not for her ardent determination to win back Mr. Darcy's good opinion, she might be in some danger.

Mitchell's liveliness of spirits and amicable manner fascinated her more than a little, and she was thankful when his older brother surrendered his place by her sister's side and joined them in want of a fresh cup of coffee.

CHAPTER 12

A CURIOUS CREATURE

To suppose Mrs. Bennet ignorant to what was unfolding before her very eyes would be akin to misunderstanding the lady's character. An attractive woman for one on the wrong side of forty, her eyes were sharp and alert to the world around her, even if her understanding was mean and often considered wanting.

Nonetheless, where it concerned one or another of her daughters and the prospect for matrimony, nothing escaped the lady's notice.

Of course, she could detect the growing fondness between her second eldest daughter and the other Mr. Hemmingsworth. To her dismay, however, Mrs. Bennet had learned the perils of counting future sons-in-law before the requisite marriage vows were exchanged.

Mrs. Bennet's favorite wish was for a double wedding at Grandover within the next three months. However, she dared not voice it aloud for she was certain Elizabeth would do anything other than see her dearest wish come true.

Obstinate, headstrong girl!

Naturally, should Bingley propose to Jane first, Mrs. Bennet was sure she would have no cause to repine. The thought of an alliance between Elizabeth and Bingley's friend also crossed her mind. However, such thoughts she dismissed as bordering on lunacy. Surely if Elizabeth and the gentleman were attracted to each other, he would have proposed by now, or so she liked to tell herself.

She scoffed. *No doubt such a proposal would be for naught, for if anyone would refuse such a man—despite it being a most advantageous alliance, what with the gentleman having ten thousand pounds a year, it would be Lizzy.*

For the time being, Mrs. Bennet's efforts were better spent secretly planning Jane's nuptials and envisioning her eldest daughter in her position as the future mistress of either Grandover or Netherfield and at least one dinner party per week in the interim, if not two.

The lady was immensely proud of herself for her family's good fortune. No other young lady in their circle could boast of having not one but two beaus—both of them charming, amicable, and rich. She always knew Jane's incredible beauty eventually would serve its purposes. As for Elizabeth, whom Mrs. Bennet considered stubborn and not nearly as tactful or as amiable as Jane, so long as she did nothing to rob her sister of the happiness Jane so richly deserved, her mother would have no cause for concern. And if by chance an alliance between Elizabeth and the younger Hemmingsworth twin should come to be, Mrs. Bennet's happiness would be almost complete.

Thoughts of the morning that awaited her spurred Elizabeth from bed. True, she would most likely see Mr. Darcy at Longbourn later that day, but spending time with him in the company of others hardly compared to spending time alone with him. It ought to have mattered to her that their private meetings would be frowned upon. Elizabeth, however, had always followed her own guiding principles. This, in her opinion, was no time to change.

After refreshing herself, her last stop before heading out the door was the kitchen. There she gathered all the usual things and loaded them into a basket, taking extra care with its presentation. Having learned how much Mr. Darcy enjoyed apples, she tossed in a couple more for good measure.

Thoughts of the day before brought a smile to her face. She recalled teasingly offering him a bite of one of hers. Rather than take it in his hand, he seized her hand, brought it to his lips, and then took a big bite of Elizabeth's apple. Wet and juicy, and for an instant, his lips met with her fingers. Utterly delectable.

A tremor of excitement coursed through her body, just as it had before—just as it always did whenever she entertained thoughts of being alone with Mr. Darcy.

Catching herself deep in silent reverie, Elizabeth glanced at her watch. Finally, she grabbed the basket and headed for the door. The last thing in the world she wanted was to be late for that morning's assignation. Who knew horse riding lessons could be so stimulating?

An eager smile etched across Elizabeth's face.

Then, as she was preparing to leave, Mrs. Hill—the housekeeper—caught her at the kitchen doorway.

"Is everything all right, Miss Lizzy?"

Elizabeth froze in place. What must Mrs. Hill think of her? The master's daughter in the kitchen, acting the part of a servant while bearing the countenance of a schoolgirl.

Half startled, half anxious, Elizabeth laughed at this version of herself eerily reminiscent of Kitty or Lydia.

For a moment, Mrs. Hill did not seem to know what to make of this picture of Elizabeth.

"Oh, I am fine," the younger woman finally managed. "I am off for my early morning ramble. I thought I might prepare a light repast in case I return too late for breakfast with the others."

A knowing smile appeared on the housekeeper's face. She nodded. "Yes, you would not want to interrupt your outing merely to sate your morning appetite. Do hurry, for one must not tarry when such a pleasurable excursion yet awaits."

Mr. Darcy watched and waited patiently as Elizabeth drew closer. Then, when he could, he reached for the basket. "I see you brought our morning feast once again, Miss Elizabeth."

"I believe the least I can do is nourish you, sir."

He lifted the lid long enough for a quick glimpse inside. A pleasant floral scent flooded his senses, a consequence of the tiny fresh-cut bouquet Elizabeth had thought to include. "I could grow accustomed to this, you know."

Elizabeth smiled. Taking her place by his side, she asked, "What shall we do first? Shall we ride or shall we dine?"

"We must ride, of course. No doubt the exertion will do wonders in stimulating both our appetites."

"I dare not argue your point, sir. Riding it is, and as for both our appetites, I can only pray I have adequately anticipated our needs."

"Heaven forbid that we part company this morning before either of us is thoroughly satiated."

Walking along with the companion of his nightly fantasies, Darcy gave Elizabeth a sidelong glance. His gaze took in every detail of her handsome face, from her delicate, arching brows to her bewitching eyes brightened by the exertion of coming to him, to her enticing, slightly parted lips, to the pleasing tint of her cheeks gained from the cool morning air. He breathed in her scent, a sweet mixture of lavender and chamomile. All these observations were blissfully pleasing to him. He simply could not wait until he succeeded in capturing all that was yet unclaimed of her heart that he might one day make her his wife.

After that morning's ride, Darcy and Elizabeth sat beside each other on a makeshift bench, partaking in the morning's meal. Ever curious, Elizabeth broached a long-delayed topic that weighed heavily on her mind. "You never speak of the Hemmingsworths, Mr. Darcy. Why is that, if I may ask?"

Mr. Darcy shrugged. "Should I speak of them?"

"Surely you must have something to say about them. It is not as though the two are strangers to you."

"I think I know all I wish to know about them."

"Knowing you as I suspect I do, you no doubt had them investigated," Elizabeth said, half-teasingly.

Darcy said nothing, which was encouragement as well as provocation enough for Elizabeth to continue.

"Tell me that you did not have the Hemmingsworths investigated!"

"Miss Elizabeth, why must this come as a surprise?" he asked. "You know I am in love with you. Do you think for one instant that I would allow you to spend company with someone who might cause you any harm?"

"Allow me, Mr. Darcy!" Elizabeth exclaimed with

energy. "How dare you?" She stood and prepared to take her leave.

Mr. Darcy seized her hand in his, and despite her silent protest, he refused to let go. "You are an intelligent woman, Miss Elizabeth, and as you said, you know me.

"With that having been said, you are also a curious creature, are you not? Do you not want to know what I uncovered about the Hemmingsworths?"

"Not particularly," she said, wrenching her hand free.

"I will tell you all the same, for what I learned is what you no doubt already know."

He had Elizabeth's attention, as evidenced when she turned to face him.

"I discovered they are decent, upright men. No one who knows them can have any cause to complain, I am sure."

"Spoken without a hint of jealousy on your part," Elizabeth said.

"Should I be jealous, Miss Elizabeth?"

"That is for you to say, sir, not me."

"I have given you my heart—I would be a fool not to trust you with it."

"You—you trust me, Mr. Darcy?"

That Elizabeth would even broach such a question

gave him pause. "Can there be any doubt?" he asked. "Did I not confide my family's greatest secret to you?"

No longer content to suppress his desire for her, Mr. Darcy took Elizabeth's hand, raised it to his lips, and imparted a lingering kiss. Would that he could kiss her lips instead—that and more. Heaven knows how much he longed for her—he ached for her.

At length, he uttered, "I trust you with all my heart."

CHAPTER 13

A RESPECTABLE PROFESSION

"I must marry a woman with her own fortune."

Hearing this, Elizabeth nearly stumbled. She could not help but wonder what it was about second sons that compelled them to inform her of their need to marry a woman with her own fortune. First, there was Colonel Fitzwilliam, Mr. Darcy's cousin and the second son of the Earl of Matlock. Now it was Mr. Mitchell Hemmingsworth's turn.

Am I wearing a 'young lady in want of a husband' sign on my back?

In that same playful manner in which she had replied to the colonel all those weeks ago in Kent, Elizabeth asked, "Pray, what is the usual price of a younger son? Surely you would not ask above fifty thousand pounds—which I believe to be the asking price of the second son of an earl, but I do not doubt you are just as worthy."

"I know you well enough to suspect a fair amount of teasing in your sentiment, Miss Elizabeth. That said, I shall not take umbrage as my immediate future precludes me from any such prospect."

"Are you saying you are not presently in want of a wife?"

"I have yet to discuss this with my family, so I must beg for your discretion. You see, Miss Elizabeth, I am seriously considering joining the military. My mother and brother have longed wished for me to study the law, and perhaps I will, just not now."

"I suppose being in the military is a respectable profession, albeit a dangerous one."

"Which is all the more reason for me not to tell my mother, or even my brother, for that matter. Remember, this is our secret."

"How do you know I can be trusted with such a secret, sir? As wholly unconnected to each other as we are, what if my loyalties lie elsewhere?"

"And here I was relying on this undeniable bond between the two of us. Who might possibly tempt you to forsake my unwavering trust in you?"

"Let me see," Elizabeth began, "there is my dearest sister, Jane, for one. And let us not forget—"

He held up his hand in jest. "Pray, say no more, my dearest. I fear my bruised ego cannot endure it."

"Those are interesting words, to say the least, for a man who moments ago all but affirmed his lack of intentions."

"Oh, but must my limitations as a second son preclude a lasting connection between us?"

Elizabeth nearly lost her step. Noticing this, Hemmingsworth reached his hand out to steady her.

Hurrying to restore her balance as well as her equanimity, Elizabeth said, "Pray, be serious, sir."

"I am very serious, Miss Elizabeth. The lasting connection I am referring to involves an alliance between my brother and your sister."

Elizabeth exhaled.

"I suspect you might wish for an alliance between your sister and Bingley. Again, do not mistake me, Miss Elizabeth. I am sure Charles Bingley is a fine man. I have no doubt he can take excellent care of your sister. After all, happiness in marriage is a matter of chance, but there is no reason to suspect she will not be just as happy, if not more so, with a man like my brother. Of course, I should not boast of my own kin, but I would say he is one of the best men I know: upright, constant, devoted, unflappable, driven, and steadfast. And did I mention exceedingly handsome?" Here he smiled that wonderfully charming smile of his. He shrugged. "Not that I am one to judge another man's good looks."

"Why are you telling me all of this?"

"Because of your history with the gentleman at Netherfield, you may not be an ally in my brother's quest to win your sister's heart. I cannot fault you for that. I only ask that you not be a foe."

"I only want what is best for my sister. So if your brother is her choice, of course I shall embrace their union wholeheartedly. As for your being my sister's brother-in-law, as a result, I shall be delighted beyond measure. And should you enlist in the military as you plan, I cannot vouch for your safety from my younger sisters. For once you don your military regalia you will be in grave danger of both Kitty and Lydia."

Further ahead in the lane, Stanford Hemmingsworth took Jane's hand in his. The two had just exhausted the subject of Jane's past with Bingley and the likely reason for his return to his country home.

He raised her gloved hand to his lips and imparted a sweet kiss.

"There is little wonder you may be confused. I am well aware you were suffering a broken heart when we met. If you need time to consider where your heart lies, you must take all the time you need. I can imagine nothing worse than living one's life with regrets. I certainly would never wish you to suffer such a fate.

"As for me, I have never been so much in love with anyone as I am with you."

"You have known love, sir?" Jane asked, her angelic eyes imploring.

"I thought so—no doubt a youthful folly. Knowing true love has made such a difference in my life. Until you are certain of your love for me, I remain your faithful servant. I am here—I am waiting for you. I shall respect whatever decision you make."

Jane was in every way perfect for him. She was indeed the epitome of beauty and kindness. If she could not return his love, Hemmingsworth did not know what he would do. He could not imagine living his life without her.

Jane's blonde hair was as dazzling as the morning sun, her wide, round eyes the color of the sky. Her skin was delicate, fresh, and sweet, like a perfect rose, and her lips, he surely imagined, tasted as delightful as honey. In her, Stanford Hemmingsworth had found the embodiment of his entire life's hopes and dreams.

I shall persist, and one day she may very well be mine.

Hours after Mr. Hemmingsworth's amorous declaration and his tender touch, the remembrance lingered still in Jane's mind. Oh, to but know a man who professed his heart's most ardent desire with no guarantee of mutual regard on the lady's part.

Being wooed by two gentlemen—both of them handsome and amiable—was beyond Jane's wildest dreams. She told her sister Elizabeth as much that night before retiring to bed.

"I can think of no one more deserving than you, dearest Jane."

"But my indecisiveness robs me of my equanimity."

"I suppose you will have to decide between the two of your beaus at some point. However, if you were to ask for my opinion, I would say you already made your decision."

"Pray what is your opinion, dearest Lizzy?"

"I dare not say—far be it from me to put my finger on Cupid's scale."

It was just as well that Elizabeth kept her opinion

to herself. Jane had not been entirely forthcoming with her sister. Indeed, Mr. Bingley had given her the strongest hints of wanting to spend the rest of his life with her. It was all she could do to prevent him from saying the words out loud. Whether Jane was not sure she wished to spend the rest of her life with him or whether she was sure she did not want to be parted from Mr. Hemmingsworth, she could not say.

While the thought of spending her life with Charles Bingley did not offend her, the idea of being parted from Stanford Hemmingsworth was too much for her to bear.

CHAPTER 14

CAUSE FOR CONCERN

Colonel Forster's young bride and Lydia Bennet became fast friends when the militia he headed was encamped outside of Meryton. Weeks had passed since the militia had gone to Brighton. Mrs. Forster, energized by the idea of Lydia's coming to stay with her, put forth the invitation.

Despite Kitty's protests about not being included in the invitation and Elizabeth's protests against the recklessness of such an invitation to a young girl of Lydia's wild animal spirits, Lydia's protests won the day.

Mr. Bennet's abhorrence of anything that might disturb his tranquility compelled him to agree, citing that Longbourn would have no peace unless Lydia had her way.

Elizabeth was so upset over her youngest sister's impending trip to Brighton that she spoke of her distress with Mr. Darcy when they finished their early morning ride and sat beside each other on a blanket in a grassy field.

Some mention of her primary cause for concern was inevitable—the dangers of her sister being in Mr. Wickham's proximity. Owing to the letter Mr. Darcy wrote to her laying bare Mr. Wickham's loathsome character, Elizabeth really feared for her sister's safety, what with Lydia's penchant for gentlemen in red coats in general and her fondness for the lieutenant in particular.

In further speaking of the letter, Elizabeth said, "It has been a while since I read it, having committed every word to heart. I can assure you I am not proud of how I comported myself toward you before knowing the full story of Mr. Wickham's treachery; would that I could make amends for my condemnation of your character."

"Knowing that my sister's secret is safe from disclosure is the only thing I ask."

"I assure you, Mr. Darcy, your sister's secret is safe with me."

"Might I ask what became of the letter? Considering the spirit in which I wrote it, I can well imagine you balling it into your fists and tossing it into the fire upon your return to the parsonage house that day."

"On the contrary, sir."

Darcy's look spoke to his concern.

"Oh, you need not worry about its safekeeping, for I tucked it among my many letters from Jane. No one could possibly be concerned about the frequent correspondence between two sisters, I am sure."

"Although I would rather you had destroyed the letter, I am relieved to hear you exercised prudence where its safekeeping is concerned—more so because of my sister than myself for having breached etiquette in such a fashion by writing to you at all.

"That said, if you now feel that conveying some semblance of its contents is a way to persuade your father against allowing your sister to travel to Brighton, where she too might fall prey to the likes of George Wickham, I shall provide my own verbal testimony to him should you need me to do so."

"Sir, as much as I appreciate your willingness to intervene on my behalf, I fear such a sacrifice might be in vain. My father as much as laughed at me when I tried to persuade him against allowing Lydia to visit Brighton."

Elizabeth shuddered a little in recollection of her father's sardonic retort. He had gone so far as to tease of Lydia's having frightened away one of her sisters' beaus and further said, *"At any rate, she cannot grow many degrees worse without authorizing us to lock her up for the rest of her life."*

On hearing Elizabeth's recitation Darcy could not but wonder what manner of man would speak so callously about the possibility of ruination for one or more of his daughters.

He took Elizabeth's hand in his and squeezed it gently. "Let us pray then that Colonel Forster is indeed a responsible man—one who will not allow your sister to meet with any harm."

In silence, he resolved to do even better. He was not a man without means, and when it came to protecting those he loved, there was nothing he would not do. He loved Elizabeth more than he loved anyone.

Twin brothers Stanford and Mitchell Hemmingsworth had just finished horse racing across the vast meadows of Grandover Park. They now sat across from each other in the study, enjoying their drinks. After Stanford teased Mitchell over the latter's loss, a lengthy discussion ensued concerning the Bennet sisters, Jane and Elizabeth—specifically their respective intentions toward the young ladies.

"I like Miss Bennet. Indeed, I love her. I knew it from the first moment I laid eyes on her. I fully intend to make her my wife. However, we are not speaking of my feelings for Miss Bennet. We are speaking of your feelings for Miss Elizabeth."

Mitchell swirled his beverage in its glass. "As a second son, does it matter how I feel? We both know I need to marry a woman with her own fortune. There is also Miss Elizabeth's situation to be considered."

Stanford arched his brow. "Her situation?"

"I believe her heart belongs to another."

"To whom?"

"Fitzwilliam Darcy," said Mitchell, his tone hinting at his feelings on the matter.

Thinking back, Stanford had to admit he had detected symptoms of affection between Darcy and Elizabeth. But, similar to his view on Bingley's apparent affection for Jane, he did not give Darcy's feelings a great deal of thought. He rather supposed a gentleman as fastidious as Fitzwilliam Darcy—one who boasted of noble lineage—would never entertain any serious intentions for anyone beneath him in consequence. "If that is indeed the case, why has he not offered for her?"

Mitchell shrugged. "Who says he has not?"

"Supposing he has, why has she not accepted?"

He shook his head. "I would rather not speculate."

"Whatever is the case, if you like her, why not pursue her? As the wife of Mitchell Hemmingsworth, surely she would have no cause to repine."

"I only want the best for her," said Mitchell. "As for a possible connection between us, I shall content myself with being her dearest sister's brother."

Mrs. Hemmingsworth walked into the room in time to hear Mitchell's speech. "What are the two of you discussing? Are you contemplating making Miss Bennet an offer of marriage, Stanford?"

An elegant-looking woman, Mrs. Hemmingsworth was as true the protective matriarch as anyone, having raised two sons on her own after their father passed away when they were but twelve years old.

Stanford knew full well his mother's fondness for Jane and Elizabeth did not extend to the Bennets of Longbourn as a whole. However, this was not entirely without good reason. Soon after her arrival, Mrs. Hemmingsworth and her sons were invited to Lucas

Lodge. Many of the Lucases' acquaintances were present, including the Bennets.

Mrs. Bennet made no secret of her annoyance with her friend Lady Lucas for being the first to receive Mrs. Hemmingsworth. Why, everyone who knew anything knew Mr. Stanford Hemmingsworth was the rightful property of Jane. But alas, more than a few people bore witness to Mrs. Bennet's testimony, including Mrs. Hemmingsworth.

The latter had never been one to suffer fools, nor did she favor such indecorous behavior as that exhibited by the younger Bennet daughters or the cool indifference of the father. All the Bennet family's suite of deficiencies had been on full display that evening. Mrs. Hemmingsworth was appalled.

Stanford nodded. "Pray that does not meet with your disapproval."

"If she is your choice, Son, far be it from me to stand in your way."

"She is my choice, Mother. Should Miss Bennet accept my proposal, I believe it is incumbent upon you to accept her family as well, for we will all be connected."

"I said I would not oppose your marrying the young lady. What more would you have me do?"

"You must extend an invitation to her family to

dine with us here at Grandover Park as a start. Furthermore, should Mrs. Bennet extend a similar invitation for our family to dine at Longbourn, you must accept. You must stop looking for reasons to refuse her hospitality."

CHAPTER 15

IN HIS POSSESSION

One by one, Charlotte opened the books on her bookcase in her parlor. She flipped through the pages of each one of them and even turned them up and gave them a vigorous shaking, all to no avail. Each book was as empty as the one before. What a startling discovery.

"Where is it?" She flopped on the floor in the middle of more than twenty books slung about. Something was terribly amiss.

"Where on earth is it? Where is Mr. Darcy's letter to Elizabeth?"

After searching through every other book in her room, a harrowing realization descended upon her. There was only one thing to do. So Charlotte returned to the parlor, sat down at her writing desk, and began to write:

Dearest Eliza, this is one of the most difficult letters I have ever had to write, and yet it must be done. I pray you will not be too disappointed with me when you read what I must convey.

First, let me start at the beginning. Then you will understand why I have implicated my own husband in this most unfortunate scheme. Soon after you departed from Kent, I made a most startling discovery when searching through Mr. Collins's bureau in want of a fresh stack of paper. Prepare yourself for something horrible, for he had in his possession a letter written to you by Mr. Darcy. That he had stashed it away inside the bureau's back panel surely did not bode well. However, mishap and fate had conspired to lead me to its discovery when I dropped a pen on the floor.

I know not how it came to be in his possession—at first, but then I recalled having seen him quit your room on the day before you were set to depart for London. You can only imagine my surprise, for I knew the room to be unoccupied because both you and Mariah were away from the parsonage.

I immediately questioned what he was about. His response was reasonable enough. He attributed his being there to examining the shelves in the closet. He made some excuse of wanting to apprise Lady Catherine of their current condition. Of course, I did not think about it further. In hindsight, I ought to have pursued the matter.

To return to my finding the letter, I knew not why Mr. Collins had it in his possession or what he planned to do with it. I cannot say whether he read its contents, but let me assure you that I certainly did not. However, I removed the letter from its hiding place behind the bureau. I put it away for safekeeping until I could hand it over to you personally.

Oh, Eliza, you cannot imagine the extent of my mortification upon discovering just this morning that the letter is no longer where I stored it. Even worse, I can have no way of knowing how long ago it was removed.

I can only attribute the missing letter to yet another act on Mr. Collins's part. What he intends to do with it I cannot say. But, hopefully, whatever it is, the consequence will not be any actual damage to either you or Mr. Darcy, whom I understand has returned to Netherfield Park with Mr. Bingley some weeks ago.

Faithfully yours,
Charlotte Collins

Elizabeth read Charlotte's letter, and she reread it. How was this even possible? She was sure she had Mr. Darcy's letter in her possession. She had purposely tucked it inside the letters she received from Jane. She was half tempted to go through the bundle as proof of what she was absolutely sure she had done. That would, of course, have belied Charlotte's testimony.

Elizabeth searched her memory for evidence of Mr. Collins's theft. She had noticed him behaving more peculiarly than usual. She now marked its origin to soon after the Rosings guests left Kent. But why would he revert to such stratagems? How did he know to go searching for Mr. Darcy's letter? Did he come across it by happenstance, or did he deliberately search for the letter? And if the latter, how could he possibly have known of its existence?

A troubling thought entered Elizabeth's inquiring mind. Had someone observed her in the lane with Mr. Darcy? Had someone witnessed what had unfolded between them and reported back to Mr. Collins?

Elizabeth gasped!

Did Mr. Collins see Mr. Darcy and me that day? Did he go in search of the letter Mr. Darcy handed me, and if so, to what end? Does he mean to use Mr. Darcy's letter against me?

Elizabeth really did not know how to think or how to feel in the face of these possibilities. Mr. Darcy had placed an extraordinary degree of trust in her by writing the things he did in the letter.

What will he say—what will he think when he learns I mishandled his most guarded family secrets?

The most damaging part of Mr. Darcy's letter came to her mind:

"I must now mention a circumstance which I would wish to forget myself, and which no obligation less than the present should induce me to unfold to any human being. Having said thus much, I feel no doubt of your secrecy.

My sister, who is more than ten years my junior, was left to the guardianship of my mother's nephew, Colonel Fitzwilliam, and myself. Then, about a year ago, she was taken from school, and an establishment was formed for her in London. Last summer, she went with the lady who presided over it to Ramsgate.

Thither also went Mr. Wickham, undoubtedly by design, for there proved to have been a prior acquaintance between him and Mrs. Younge, in whose character we were most unhappily deceived. By her connivance and aid, he so far recommended himself to Georgiana, whose affectionate heart retained a strong impression of his kindness to her as a child, that she was persuaded to believe herself in love and to consent to an elopement.

She was then but fifteen, which must be her excuse, and after stating her imprudence, I am happy to add that I owed the knowledge of it to herself. I joined them unexpectedly a day or two before the intended elopement. Then Georgiana, unable to support the idea of grieving and offending a brother whom she almost looked up to as a father, acknowledged the whole to me. You may imagine what I felt and how I acted. Regard for my sister's credit and feelings prevented any public exposure.

This recollection caused Elizabeth some distress.

No doubt, upon hearing of all this, Mr. Darcy will distrust me—or, even worse, detest me.

Foolish, foolish girl. How could I have been so careless? I ought to have destroyed the letter the first chance I got. So why on earth did I keep it?

No matter how many questions she asked, no matter how many answers she lacked, Elizabeth knew there was only one thing to be done. It was untenable that the information in the letter might one day come back to haunt either of them, especially Mr. Darcy.

I must tell him everything when I see him again. I pray he will not hate me for my betrayal of his trust.

CHAPTER 16

MAKING MATTERS WORSE

Being the co-guardian of a sister more than a decade his junior meant the shouldering of profound responsibility for a single man. Although by his design, his young sister, Georgiana, had her own establishment in town, Mr. Darcy still provided what he considered prodigious care of her. He surely had failed her when he hired Mrs. Younge to oversee his sister and allowed them to travel to Ramsgate. Nevertheless, he was confident she was safe in her new companion's care. Not only had Mrs. Annesley been recommended by his aunt Lady Fitzwilliam, the wife of his uncle, the Earl of Matlock, but Darcy had subjected the woman to an intense background investigation.

Ever since the Ramsgate fiasco, Darcy made sure to

maintain regular written correspondence with Georgiana whenever he was away from town, which, owing to his style of living, was more frequent than not. During the past year alone, he had spent more than half of it in Kent, Somersetshire, and Hertfordshire. Time spent away from town was not without good reason, especially of late. Winning Miss Elizabeth Bennet's hand in marriage was his greatest wish.

However, he had not received a letter from his sister in nearly two weeks, which meant she was three in his deficit. At first, he had thought to return to London to determine, in person, why Georgiana had returned none of his letters, but he later persuaded himself to write a letter to Mrs. Annesley instead. It would not have been the first time he implored such means to ascertain his young sister's state of mind.

Mrs. Annesley's response was swift. It bore anything but the type of news Darcy was hoping for—information perhaps that his young sister was so busily engaged in activities such as painting, drawing, spending time with friends, and practicing the pianoforte that writing to an older brother had suffered. Instead, he learned Georgiana had been removed from London—that she was living under Lady Catherine de Bourgh's protection and by Mr. Darcy's design.

Making matters worse, a missive from Lady Catherine herself was in Darcy's possession—one he had received a while ago. He had placed it aside for his later perusal, suspecting as he did it was yet another letter from his aunt haranguing him to honor his duty to her daughter Anne by marrying her. Was there any wonder the letter had escaped his mind?

Darcy retrieved the letter from the drawer and tore open the seal. He pored over his aunt's scribblings in horror. She knew! The Ramsgate affair, Georgiana's near brush with scandal, George Wickham's treachery. Lady Catherine knew it all. Moreover, she meant to use this knowledge to her greatest advantage, accusing Darcy of the dereliction of his duties in the co-guardianship of his sister for neglecting her and placing her in the care of those who would subject her to peril, derision, and censorship were the information widely known.

Unless Darcy honored his obligation to the Fitzwilliam family by marrying Anne, Lady Catherine would use the information she had against him to strip him of his role as Georgiana's co-guardian.

This will not do! How dare my own flesh and blood attempt to threaten me? Lady Catherine, this time you have gone too far!

Darcy started crumpling the letter in his fist until

he thought better of it. He needed the letter intact to serve as evidence of his own—should matters later dictate it. He would never marry Anne against his will or anyone else for that matter. How could he when he had pledged his heart and soul to Elizabeth? His sole purpose in being in Hertfordshire was to be near her, so he might stand a chance of winning hers.

Circumstances beyond his control had now conspired to force his removal from that part of the country in order to handle his aunt.

However, a promised outing with Elizabeth meant delaying his leave-taking, at least by an hour. Even amid such a disturbing crisis as this, he simply had to see her.

Soon afterward, Darcy was pacing the lane, the tumult of his mind evident. Unanswered questions plagued his thoughts, the most pressing being how Lady Catherine had learned of the Ramsgate affair in the first place?

Elizabeth was eager to see Mr. Darcy, and for a good reason. The sooner she informed him of the missing letter the better. Even if Mr. Collins had not used the intelligence against them, there was no guarantee he would not. Otherwise, he had stolen the letter for nothing, and what were the chances of that?

When she saw him, she noticed his usually reserved manner was altered. He rushed over to her.

"Miss Elizabeth, I am glad you have come. I have something I need to discuss with you. It is a subject that cannot be delayed. You see—"

Elizabeth said, "Mr. Darcy, I fear I must beg your indulgence, for what I have to say is of the utmost importance. May I speak first?"

"Yes—yes, of course."

Elizabeth immediately recounted the letter from her friend. Mr. Darcy stared. He said nothing, although his pained expression spoke volumes. Elizabeth waited in wretched suspense.

At length, Mr. Darcy said, "Miss Elizabeth, I know we spoke of the letter, and you told me you had not destroyed it. You gave me your assurance the letter was safely concealed and, more importantly, within your possession."

Elizabeth bore a look of deep contrition. "I am sorry, sir."

Taking a deep breath, Darcy turned his head and stared off into the distance. At length, he looked back at her. He swallowed hard. "If only you had destroyed it."

Before Elizabeth could fashion a response, he said, "I put all my trust in you—"

Elizabeth thought she saw what she feared was disappointment in his eyes—a look that told her all she needed to know. Mr. Darcy no longer trusted her. She had lost his good opinion. She could not help but demure in remembrance of his solemn testimony that his good opinion once lost was lost forever.

"Sir—"

He held up his hand. "I cannot—I dare not...."

Deeply absorbed in their conversation, Darcy and Elizabeth were caught unaware by the arrival of a third party.

"Miss Elizabeth?"

Startled, Elizabeth turned to face the speaker.

"Mr. Hemmingsworth," she said, disappointed but not entirely surprised, for upon learning of her early morning rides with Mr. Darcy, Mitchell would sometime arrive on his own horse, bent on accompanying them.

Mitchell sprung from his horse. Then, drawing nearer, he asked, "Is everything all right?"

Elizabeth looked at Mr. Darcy—her eyes questioning.

"I will leave you now, Miss Elizabeth," said Mr. Darcy, his voice cool and unaffected.

"Sir?"

"As I meant to explain earlier, I … I have urgent matters to attend away from Hertfordshire. I will take my leave of you." He bowed. "Good day, Miss Elizabeth." He turned and walked away—long strides forcing them farther and farther apart, and although Elizabeth stood frozen in place, looking at him disappear from her life, not once did he turn and look back.

Once Mr. Darcy had disappeared entirely from sight, Mr. Hemmingsworth asked, "What was that about, Miss Elizabeth? You look upset."

Fearing that she had fallen from Mr. Darcy's favor due to her careless handling of his letter, Elizabeth's eyes welled with tears. She said nothing.

"Miss Elizabeth," Mr. Hemmingsworth began, "have the two of you suffered some misunderstanding?"

She nodded her head. Still, she was silent.

"Whatever it is, I am certain it can be resolved. The two of you care for each other."

Mr. Darcy's edict on his character echoed in Elizabeth's mind once more: *"My good opinion once lost is lost forever."*

Refusing his hand in marriage in the uncivil manner that she did was one thing, even justified, owing to the ungentlemanly way in which he offered it. However, risking the exposure of a closely held family secret owing to her own neglect—one that threatened his sister's good name—was an entirely different and likely an unforgivable matter altogether.

"No," Elizabeth said, shaking her head. "I fear, this time, Mr. Darcy is lost to me forever."

"Surely not," Hemmingsworth began, "why would you entertain such thoughts?"

"I cannot help but feel I have lost his good opinion once and for all."

"Surely it cannot be as bad as you think. He seems very fond of you, even a bit possessive," said her ever-steadfast companion.

"Yes, but this is not the first time I have given him cause for disappointment. More than that, he prides himself on being unforgiving by nature.

"What if I have trifled with his affections for too

long and he has simply given up on me?" Elizabeth mused out loud.

Hemmingsworth was right there by her side, assuring her that such was not the case. "Surely Mr. Darcy cares for you—no doubt he loves you deeply. There must be another reason for his leaving."

However, a young woman with the distinction of being crossed in love was unlikely to be so easily consoled. Mr. Darcy's apparent defection was really something to think of—thoughts best entertained in private.

In silence, Elizabeth considered she must find a way to regain Mr. Darcy's trust. She wondered, further, how such a task was to be accomplished should she never see him again.

CHAPTER 17

SINISTER FORCES

LONDON, ENGLAND – DARCY HOUSE

*D*arcy and his cousin Colonel Fitzwilliam sat across from each other, deep in solemn deliberation. Undoubtedly, a fair amount of liquor had been consumed by the two of them. Darcy had never been more disgusted with a family member's conduct. Copious liquor consumption was a balm for his battered spirits.

He set his empty glass aside and regarded his cousin with intent. "It ought to go without asking, but in my search for answers, I believe I ought to leave no stone unturned."

Finishing up his own drink, the colonel asked, "What is your question?"

"Pray, tell me you knew nothing of Lady Catherine's scheme to strip me of my authority over Georgiana."

"You have my word. Indeed, I knew nothing other than Georgiana was in Kent with our aunt by your design."

"I can very well imagine Lady Catherine told everyone that I approved of my sister being in Kent, including Georgiana herself, as a means of concealing her true intentions."

"Yet, Lady Catherine has not taken legal action. Else I surely would have been notified as Georgiana's co-guardian," the colonel said.

"Legally, what can she do so long as she is attempting to use the information she has to force me to marry Anne? Once I make it perfectly clear to her that I have no intention of doing so, I imagine she will grow desperate."

"Are you willing to take such a chance when your sister's reputation is at stake?"

"Marrying Anne was never a consideration for me—despite Lady Catherine's claims that it was my mother's favorite wish. Supposing what she said is true, the two of them did their part in planning such a union, but its execution depends entirely on others. I have been my own man for far too long to bend to the will of others now.

"I will go to Kent and compel our aunt to be reasonable, as well as determine how she came about such information. For all I know, she may have learned it from Georgiana herself, although I rather doubt it, for I suspect far more sinister forces are at play."

"I am more than happy to accompany you, supposing I might be of service."

"I thank you for your offer, Cousin. However, I do not know that it is necessary. That said, I may prevail on you later, subject to what I learn in Kent about how this whole thing came about.

"I admit to discussing the Ramsgate affair with someone outside our circle, but I refuse to allow that she is the one who divulged the information. There has to be another explanation for how Lady Catherine learned about Georgiana's near brush with scandal."

"She?" the colonel asked, leaning closer and arching his brow.

"Miss Elizabeth Bennet," Darcy replied, not wishing to prolong the discussion with a long, drawn-out account of how it came to be.

The colonel's curiosity, however, would not be

repressed. "I fail to understand why you would confide such a family secret to anyone. How could you have shared this secret with someone so wholly unconnected to you?"

"It is a long story—too long to do it justice at such a critical time as this. Suffice it to say, Miss Elizabeth is more connected to me than you can possibly know."

"But in all the time I spent with the two of you in Kent, I saw no real symptoms of affection by either of you. Unless this is a recent development. Did you confide in her during your recent stay in Hertfordshire?"

"No—it was long before that."

"It could not possibly have happened before our time in Kent."

"Actually," Darcy said, "it occurred while we were in Kent—just before we took our leave. I wrote a letter to her and hand-delivered it to her in the grove that very morning."

"I am sure you do not need a lecture from me on the impropriety of such behavior."

"I am absolutely sure of that."

"You said you will not allow that Miss Elizabeth divulged the information to anyone. But perchance she may have misplaced the letter. Did you ask her about it?"

Darcy nodded. "The sad truth is she does not know what became of the letter. I believe her when she said she exercised caution in securing it. Perhaps it was lost—it may have been stolen, but as I said, I cannot allow there is a connection to my giving her the letter and our aunt learning about the Ramsgate affair."

"Because?"

"Because I love her."

Soon after Mr. Darcy withdrew from Hertfordshire, Mr. Bingley did likewise. This time, at least, the latter offered a good excuse. He planned to bring one or the other of his sisters with him when he returned so that he might have a female relation in residence to preside over his table. It seemed all the talk of the Bennets possibly being invited to dine at Grandover Park at any day had placed Bingley at a decided disadvantage—one he could easily overcome now that the London season was at an end. His sisters would be eager to be away from town.

Jane further informed Elizabeth that according to Bingley, Darcy left because his aunt had taken custody of Georgiana and she had information that might prove detrimental to Darcy—conceivably information of his negligence as the co-guardian of a sister more than a decade his junior.

All too aware of Elizabeth's low spirits and the reason, Jane said, "So you see, dearest Lizzy, his leave-taking cannot possibly be because of anything you may have said or done."

This information was terrible to Elizabeth's way of thinking. Did she dare mention her fear of being the means of Lady Catherine de Bourgh's attempt to bend her nephew to her will?

No—she could not. *This would be yet another violation of his trust,* she considered.

Wanting to discuss anything with her sister other than Mr. Darcy's private affairs, Elizabeth sought to change the subject.

"What of Mr. Bingley's return? Did he give you a definitive date?"

"No, he did not. Nor did I press him for one."

"No," Elizabeth said, "I do not suppose you would have—not after what happened last Nov—" Here, she paused. The last thing she wanted to do was injure her dearest sister by reminding her of Mr. Bingley's inconstancy.

Jane knew and understood what her sister was about. "Lizzy, you do not have to censor your speech with me. I have forgiven Mr. Bingley for his behavior, after all. I certainly do not mean to suffer the remembrance of it with agony and regret. On the whole, the gentleman owes me nothing."

Elizabeth said, "Jane?"

"I speak nothing but the truth. For all I know, Mr. Bingley's return may be precipitated on the whim of one or the other of his sisters. But whatever he decides, I do not mean to make myself anxious about it."

"I suppose you make a good point. For, after all, with so much to entertain with the goings-on at Grandover Park, why indeed would you?"

Elizabeth knew her sister better than anyone. Jane said nothing in reply to her sister's retort. She did not need to, for her sentiments were written all over her face. Jane was more than halfway in love with Mr. Stanford Hemmingsworth by now, even if she had yet to admit it to herself.

CHAPTER 18

THE GENERAL UNDERSTANDING

KENT, ENGLAND—ROSINGS PARK

The formidable confrontation was well underway. Before arriving in Kent, Darcy had consulted a team of solicitors. He knew exactly what he was about.

Neither his aunt nor he was willing to concede. Both were determined to carry their points.

"You would air our family's secrets in such a public manner?"

"If you care anything about our family, you will not force my hand in this matter," Lady Catherine countered.

"What kind of mother are you to wish for such an

unhappy alliance for your only daughter? Surely you believe Anne is worthy of marrying a man who loves her."

"What does love have to do with anything? People in our sphere marry for wealth, for power, for connections. That is the way of our world, and the sooner you accept it the better for everyone involved." Lady Catherine scoffed. "Why on earth do you think your mother and I planned the union between our two children, you and Anne, at your birth, if not for the general understanding of the rules and expectations of our society?

"Why do you think your mother married your father?" She scoffed again. "The daughter of an earl married to a gentleman who was not a peer! My father allowed the marriage because of the Darcy fortune. Do not pretend to suppose otherwise.

"That is even more reason why my brother the Earl of Matlock will side with me should I pursue the matter of Georgiana's guardianship. She may be merely the daughter of a gentleman, but she is the granddaughter of a peer. Moreover, under your supervision, she came shockingly close to eloping with a reprobate—a vile creature of the lowest kind.

"Well, I shall not risk it again. Under my supervision, or the supervision of my Anne once she has assumed her place as the mistress of Pemberley, Georgiana will finally receive the guidance and attention a young woman of her standing ought to receive. She will no longer be randomly handed off from one hired woman to the next merely for the sake of your convenience."

"Once and for all, Lady Catherine, I will not marry Anne. Do not dare use my sister as a pawn in your scheme to force my hand under the pretense of wanting what is best for her! Had my father wanted you to be my sister's guardian, then he would not have left her to my care—mine and the colonel's."

Her ladyship laughed. "Your late father was not infallible. Otherwise, he would not have made Wickham his godson. I contend his naming you and your cousin as Georgiana's co-guardians was yet another example of his poor judgment."

"How dare you impugn my father's character merely to advance your selfish scheme?"

Lady Catherine drew closer and pointed her bejeweled walking stick at Darcy's face. "I will do whatever it takes to carry my point. You know me, Nephew. You know the frankness of my character. I am not used to having my will thwarted by others. You ought to know what I am capable of."

Darcy did not flinch. "And you, Lady Catherine, ought to know me!"

As much as Darcy did not wish to remain in Kent a moment longer than was necessary, spending several days with his sister was paramount. If he had learned anything of late, it was the importance of spending time with her.

Their frequent correspondence was not a substitute for his being with her as an older brother and as a co-guardian. Knowing that his decisions played a part in his sister's desire to remain at Rosings distressed him beyond measure.

"I do not blame you for my situation, nor do I expect you to arrange the business of your life around mine. But why would I want to have my own establishment when I might best spend my time with family?" Georgiana asked, walking along beside her older brother in the beautifully manicured lane.

"I do not understand," Darcy confessed to his sister. "Of all the possible arrangements, why do you wish to remain in Kent?"

"Have you not always stressed the importance of

family?" Georgiana asked. "And despite our aunt's eccentricities, Lady Catherine is my family.

"What is more, there are so few of us on the paternal side, not one that I know is my age. As for our maternal relations, there are fewer still. Cousin Anne is the only one who might be deemed close to me in age. Not only that, the two of us have been getting along very well since my time here in Kent. We have grown closer, so much so that you might consider us is more than cousins but rather as intimate friends."

"Pray you do not agree with Lady Catherine that Anne and I should marry."

"Why on earth would I want to see Anne suffer a loveless marriage? Surely our cousin deserves better. Both of you do."

"Georgiana, the truth is I dislike you living with our aunt. I know better than you what she is about. I do not like her using you as a pawn in her scheme to force my hand to marry Anne."

"How might she possibly do that, given how determined you are against the scheme?"

Darcy drew a sharp breath. "Prepare yourself for disappointment. You see, Lady Catherine knows about what happened in Ramsgate. She knows it all. She threatens to use the intelligence to remove you from my guardianship if I do not do what she wants. I am sorry to have to tell you this. And I am even sorrier that I may have been the means of Lady Catherine's discovering your secret."

"You?" Georgiana asked. Before Darcy could say more, she said, "No, you see, Brother, I am Lady Catherine's source. I told Anne all about what happened in Ramsgate. No doubt, she told her mother."

"Knowing Lady Catherine's plan, do you understand why I cannot tolerate her having a role in your life?"

"I do not doubt that our aunt's stance reflects a sort of desperation. But on the whole, I believe it would not be good to hold that against Anne, who has already suffered enough.

"Brother, you and I both know that nothing on earth will make you marry Anne. As for my guardianship, I do not believe Lady Catherine will force your hand, for she will have nothing to gain by doing so and everything to lose. If she persists, I shall simply invite Anne to live with me in my establishment in town. I know our aunt will not risk alienating all three of us."

"It seems you have given this some thought. When did you become so wise?"

"Surely living with my aunt must have some

advantages. But that said, why on earth do you believe you bore any responsibility in Lady Catherine learning my secret?"

"Let me just say it is a long story, one I do not wish to explain just now—not until I have all the facts," said Darcy. "However, I would ask one more thing of you."

"What is that?"

"My recent departure from Hertfordshire was rather abrupt, to say the least. If I have not made a complete shamble of things and events unfold as I hope, my life, as I know it, will undergo a major change. Should I prevail, I hope you will consider making Pemberley your home."

"Fitzwilliam, are you suggesting what I think you are?"

"That depends on what you are thinking I am suggesting."

"Are you hoping to marry?"

Darcy said nothing. He merely smiled.

"You do not have to tell me. I do not suppose you are spending as much time in Hertfordshire as you do of late for nothing."

CHAPTER 19

MORE INCONVENIENT TIME

*L*ongbourn was in turmoil. It could not have happened at a more inconvenient time. The Bennets and the Hemmingsworths had just adjourned to the dining room when a servant hurried inside bearing word of Colonel Forster's untimely arrival requesting an audience with Mr. Bennet.

Thomas Bennet was less than pleased to hear of the unexpected visitor, but he could hardly refuse the summons. As his youngest daughter was under the colonel's supervision in Brighton, he could only suppose the gentleman was there with a report of her conduct. It would not have surprised him one bit to hear the officer had grown weary of such onerous employment and was eager to have Lydia return home.

Upon excusing himself from the table and joining the colonel inside the library, Longbourn's patriarch quickly learned his family's life as they knew it was over.

The colonel's report rattled even Thomas Bennet. He could hardly countenance the news and could scarcely bring himself to speak.

Lydia had run away from Brighton with one of the men in the colonel's regiment—a Lieutenant Wickham. The wayward couple was rumored to have headed to Gretna Green, but the colonel, relying on the report of a more trusted member of his regiment, knew they had not.

Bennet and Forster considered all the options available to them—none of them good considering the circumstances. A young girl who had thrown herself in the power of such a man, even if recovered, was ruined forever unless the villain could be tracked down and forced to marry her. But, as imprudent as the marriage between Mr. Wickham and poor Lydia would be, the alternative was unthinkable.

As each minute passed, it became clear the situation was grave. Something had to be done, but what? Finally, Colonel Forster took his leave with the explanation that he would do everything he could, but Mr. Bennet was without hope.

Soon, Mr. Bennet's long absence from the dining room could not be ignored. Everyone who knew him knew he liked to keep himself to himself, but that evening was special. After putting off the visit for so long as she did, Mrs. Hemmingsworth was finally persuaded to take a family dinner at Longbourn. The success of that evening would surely bode well for Jane. It was a matter of some consideration on everyone's part. Everyone was on their best behavior.

Bad news, however, by its very nature has a way of getting out, and it was not too long before everyone in Longbourn Village learned of what Lydia had done.

Mrs. Hemmingsworth was disgusted, and she could not wait to be away from Longbourn.

Then a few days later saw another wrinkle in young Lydia's plight. Among other items, a letter arrived from Wickham. It was redirected from Brighton to Longbourn by Mrs. Forster with another missive indicating she found it among the things Lydia had left behind, along with yet another letter from Lydia to Kitty asking the latter to oversee the mending of a great slit in the former's worked muslin gown. Mrs. Forster even remembered to include the tattered garment.

Elizabeth and Jane were with their father when the parcel arrived from Brighton, and they were among the first to hear when he read the letter aloud:

My darling Lydia, it pains me to distress you, but circumstances have dictated I need to take my leave of Brighton post haste. I beg of you, my dearest, to forgive me for the unkept promises we made. Please forget every tender word that was ever spoken. I further ask that you forgive me for taking advantage of your innocence. I shall forever treasure the memory of you. Your lively spirits and youthful beauty are such that you will surely find the kind of love you so richly deserve—a loving home with a husband and a household of adoring children ... everything. My regret is that you could not have those things with me. Yours forever, Lieutenant Wickham, Esq.

The sudden appearance of such a letter threw the family into even more disarray. What could be its meaning? All evidence had pointed to Lydia leaving Brighton with the scoundrel. Yet, the letter, for all intents and purposes, exonerated the lieutenant.

Was the letter real? Or was it merely part of Wickham's diabolical plan to continue their sordid affair while covering his tracks?

The tender words of a scoundrel! How disgusting. Elizabeth reread the letter several times before concluding that if it did indeed contain the truth and the lieutenant truly was innocent, what had become of Lydia? Elizabeth could not help but despair.

It was a consolation of sorts that Lady Catherine's source of Georgiana's secret was not the letter Darcy had written to Elizabeth. But that the letter's whereabouts remained unaccounted for was untenable. Darcy planned one last visit before leaving that part of the country—the parsonage.

On the way there, Darcy could not believe the madness unfolding just ahead of him.

What was William Collins thinking by escaping the lane in desperate want of a place to hide upon glimpsing Mr. Darcy? Mr. Collins was not a small man. It would take more than a couple of bushes to conceal him. Add to that, he wore a tall hat.

Darcy halted in front of Collins's hiding place.

"You have something that belongs to me."

The other man remained silent.

"Mr. Collins!"

Slowly, the ridiculous man stood with his hands raised midway in the air. He grinned awkwardly, cowardly stepping forward. Then, lowering one hand, he reached into his pocket and retrieved the stolen missive.

His voice trembling, rivaling his hand, Collins asked, "Mr. Darcy, sir, would you believe me if I told you I stumbled across this accidentally and I was just on my way to Rosings to give it to you personally before you took your leave?"

"No!" Darcy said, unceremoniously snatching the letter. "No, I do not believe you." Then, after a brief perusal, he tucked the letter inside his own pocket. Darcy had never been generous in his opinion of William Collins. However, he never supposed the vicar capable of committing theft.

"Why you would wish to make an enemy of me is beyond comprehension."

"No, sir. You misunderstand me. I only meant to protect you and my cousin."

Darcy glared at the silly man.

"Why—I…" Collins continued, "As my cousin was here in Kent under my protection, I considered it my duty to make certain that she was not bringing scandal down upon herself. I assure you, sir, that I would never have willingly exposed your family to derision."

Darcy scoffed. "On the contrary, I understand you perfectly well. I rather suspect your motives were more self-serving than benevolent."

"You are angry, and rightfully so. But I believe your anger will cease when you hear all I have to say. Then, indeed, I believe some semblance of gratitude on your part will be warranted."

"Gratitude?"

"Indeed, I, for one, congratulate myself."

"What are you going on about, man?"

"I speak of the terrible scandal that has befallen Miss Elizabeth's family. Her youngest sister, Miss Lydia, has left all her friends. By all accounts, she has eloped, throwing herself into the power of—of Lt. George Wickham. They were said to have gone off together from Brighton. There can be little doubt of the man's true intentions. The girl has no money, no connections, nothing that can tempt him to marry her. She is indeed lost forever."

Darcy listened as Elizabeth's relation continued speaking of the incident.

Grieved and shocked, he asked, "But is it certain—absolutely certain?"

"Oh, yes!" Collins exclaimed with energy and resumed conveying the details as best he understood them. His source, of course, was his wife, and her source was her mother, Lady Lucas, whose source was everyone who knew anything in Hertfordshire.

Lowering his voice, the parson said, "There have

also been reports that young Lydia may have stolen away of her own volition, believing herself to be in love."

"And what has been done? What has been attempted to recover her?"

"My cousin Mr. Bennet went to London to beg his brother's assistance. But nothing can be done. I know very well that nothing can be done as Lydia is undoubtedly living in sin. How is such a man to be worked on? How are they even to be discovered? The Bennets have not the smallest hope. It is in every way horrible!"

Darcy had heard enough. He was gone directly.

Amid all the confusion and uncertainty at Longbourn, Stanford Hemmingsworth proposed to Jane, thus offering her hope despite Lydia's situation and the horrendous scandal because of it.

He loved her too much. He had built his whole world around her. He did not mean to lose the love of his life and all his hopes for his future felicity on account of the actions of a foolish, selfish girl who cared for none other than herself.

Jane voiced her reservations. "How can I possibly

say yes when my family's reputation is ruined? I dare not. I will not bring scandal upon your family."

"My dearest Jane, I love you. Indeed, no one is loved more than I love you. No one is wanted more. Whatever you do, do not say no. Say you will think about it."

"I will be thinking about it. I shall think about it every minute of every hour of every day. But—I…"

Hemmingsworth looked deeply into Jane's eyes. "Please—no buts… I am as devoted to you as I can be. I will not let you go."

"But what of your family? How can they want to have anything to do with us after what Lydia has done? Surely they will never forgive me. You must not risk the loss of everything you hold dear. Do you think society will ever want to have anything to do with you should Lydia never be recovered and her reputation—our family's reputation—remain in tatters?"

"I do not care about society. My family loves you. They would not want or expect me to forsake you."

Jane smiled. Her eyes sparkled. Mr. Hemmingsworth had offered her a modicum of hope amid a raging storm, and her affection for him increased a thousandfold.

CHAPTER 20

SENSE OF HONOR

Lydia was discovered and recovered by way of her marriage to none other than Mr. Wickham himself. And now the newlyweds had descended upon Longbourn—two lovers as happy as could be with nary a care or a morsel of remorse between them.

The Bennets ought to have been happy with this turn of events, and indeed most of them were. However, Elizabeth most certainly was not—she was horrified and disgusted. She could not wait for the Wickhams to be on their way.

One morning, soon after their arrival, while sitting with her two elder sisters, Mrs. Wickham said to Elizabeth, "Lizzy, I never gave you an account of my wedding, I believe. You were not by when I told Mamma and the others all about it. Are you not curious to hear how it was managed?"

"No—not really," replied Elizabeth. "I think there cannot be too little said on the subject."

"La! You are so strange! But I must tell you how it went off."

Lydia began speaking. Indeed, she talked and talked, but nothing she said would pierce Elizabeth's determination to ignore the silly girl. That was until she heard Lydia mention the one person who was sure to animate her older sister—Mr. Darcy.

"Mr. Darcy!" repeated Elizabeth in utter amazement.

"Oh, yes! He was to come there with Wickham, you know. But gracious me! I quite forgot! I ought not to have said a word about it. I promised them so faithfully! What will Wickham say? It was to be such a secret!"

"If it was to be a secret," said Jane, "say not another word on the subject. You may depend upon my seeking no further."

"Oh! Certainly," said Elizabeth, though burning with curiosity, "we will ask you no questions."

"Thank you," said Lydia, "for if you did, I should

certainly tell you all, and then Wickham would be angry."

On such encouragement to ask, Elizabeth forced herself to put it out of her power by running away.

However, to live in ignorance on such a point was impossible; or at least it was impossible not to try for information. Mr. Darcy had been at her sister's wedding.

Elizabeth was too curious a creature not to wish to know more. She was too rational a creature to suppose that if what Lydia had said was true—that Mr. Darcy had helped to bring the marriage about and in so doing been the means of saving the Bennet family's reputation—he had done it all for her.

Needing answers to her questions, Elizabeth set off to write to her aunt in town. Surely her aunt would know, and then Elizabeth would know too.

She began the missive with all the usual civilities before addressing her most pressing concern:

"You must comprehend my eagerness to know how a person unconnected with any of us—a comparative stranger to our family—should have been amongst you at such a time. Pray write instantly, and let me understand it—unless it is, for very cogent reasons, to remain in the secrecy Lydia seems to think necessary. And then I must endeavor to be

satisfied with ignorance. Not that I shall, though. My dear aunt, if you do not tell me in an honorable manner, I shall certainly be reduced to tricks and stratagems to find it out."

Jane's delicate sense of honor would not allow her to speak to Elizabeth privately of what Lydia had let fall. Elizabeth was glad of it. Till it appeared whether her inquiries would receive any satisfaction, she had rather be without a confidante.

She received an answer to her letter soon thereafter. She hurried into the little grove where she was least likely to be disturbed. She sat down on the bench and prepared to be happy, for the length of the letter convinced her it did not contain a denial.

Indeed, there was no denial. On the contrary, it was precisely as Lydia had said. Mrs. Gardiner confirmed in her reply that Mr. Darcy had certainly done everything. He discovered the couple, paid off Wickham's debts, attended the wedding, and paid for Wickham's commission in the north.

Elizabeth was now at liberty to think all Mr. Darcy had done, he had done for her, but why had he done it? She had every reason to believe she had lost his good opinion when she forfeited his trust. And he had not returned. Surely any future path must lie through him.

This longing she suffered was not new to her, for it had been coming on for a long time. She honestly felt that she loved Mr. Darcy, and now more than ever before. Surely such tender feelings on her part must not be in vain.

CHAPTER 21

HER MATERNAL FEELINGS

Jane hated the idea of disappointing Mr. Bingley. But what was to be done? She could not tell her heart what to do. Even if she could, she could not persuade herself into believing the feelings she had for her former suitor could be compared to what she now felt for Mr. Hemmingsworth.

Her former suitor indeed, for that is what he was—had always been since the moment Mr. Hemmingsworth came into her life.

Mr. Bingley was my first love, she silently considered. *But, perchance, that is all he was ever meant to be. A first love. For if he was meant to be my only love, then why does my heart despair at the thought of being parted from Mr. Hemmingsworth?*

For some time, I have known I can get along perfectly fine without Mr. Bingley. I do not know that I would ever wish to find out what it is like to get along without Stanford. But what if I were to lose him? What a shame it would be if it was because I failed to show him my true feelings.

Experience had proved a good teacher. What she had found with Mr. Hemmingsworth was genuine love, constant love, mature love. The kind of love she deserved with a man who had filled all the emptiness inside her and given her life a new purpose.

On the heels of Bingley's retreat, Jane stole away for a private tête-à-tête with the true object of her affections—Stanford Hemmingsworth.

She insisted he ask her to marry him again. He did so with alacrity. Jane was to be his wife. On this happy occasion, the two lovers confirmed their long-suppressed desire for each other as violently as a newly betrothed couple could be supposed to do.

At length, the temporary cessation of their passions was absolutely necessary. There was too much to say and too much to do, starting with sharing their happiness with their loved ones.

Happy for all her maternal feelings, Mrs. Bennet knew precisely how to act. In no time at all, a lavish dinner party with all her friends and neighbors got underway at Longbourn. Even Mrs. Hemmingsworth could not refuse the invitation. She had always loved Jane, and now she loved her even more.

Elizabeth could not have been happier for her sister. At last, Jane had found the love she so richly deserved. Yet, even so, she was unequal to the festive air inside the halls of Longbourn for more than a little at a time owing to her own situation, so Elizabeth made her way outside.

Mitchell Hemmingsworth found her in the garden, gazing into the night sky. It was awash with endless galaxies, a brilliant spectrum whirling infinite miles away. The moon above gleamed down on her. There could be no doubt of where her thoughts tended. The love of her life seemed just as distant.

"Are you wishing on a star, Miss Elizabeth?" he asked, draping a light shawl over her shoulders and adjusting it just so.

Elizabeth half-smiled. She said nothing.

"It is rare to find you at a loss for words, Miss Elizabeth."

"Are you done?" she finally asked.

Mitchell shook his head. "I will not always be around to suffer such abuse, you know."

"Does that mean you have resolved to join the military?" Elizabeth asked.

He nodded. "Will you miss me?"

"I think you know the answer to that question, sir."

"I think I would like to hear it."

Elizabeth sighed wistfully. "All the time. Always."

The gentleman had no answer to that. Instead, he said, "He will return to Hertfordshire soon."

"If only I shared your optimism."

The reasons for Mr. Darcy not to return were diminishing by the day. Yes, he had been the means of saving her family from ruin when he discovered Lydia and forced Wickham to marry the silly girl, but to be the brother of such a man. It was inconceivable.

"You can always take matters into your own hands."

"What do you mean?"

"London is but a few hours away. Go there and let it be known you are in town. No doubt, he will come to Gracechurch Street once he knows you are there."

"My relations travel in such different circles than his. I cannot imagine how it could be done."

"Then go to Grosvenor Square—"

Elizabeth gasped. "I cannot possibly do such a

thing. Just how bold do you think I am, sir? I fear there is a stark difference between optimism and recklessness."

Mitchell shrugged. "Perhaps a healthy mixture of both is what is called for."

"Sir, I shall not go to London in the hope of seeing Mr. Darcy."

"Then write a letter to him."

"I do not know that I can do that either."

"Why in heavens not?" he asked daringly. "And do not dare mention the impropriety of a single person writing to another single person of the opposite sex. That is, after all, how this whole thing started, is it not?"

CHAPTER 22

IN THAT MANNER

All of Mitchell Hemmingsworth's insistence that Elizabeth should take matters into her own hands by going to town, fortunately proved for naught. Mr. Darcy returned to Hertfordshire, came directly to Longbourn, and discreetly prevailed on Elizabeth for a private audience when he could do so.

The following day found Darcy and Elizabeth at their usual place, bright and early at sunrise. Words were inadequate to express how either of them really felt being together again, but some conversation was essential. Mr. Darcy needed to account for his sudden leave-taking.

"I went to Kent thinking my sister was living at Rosings because she was forced to live there," he explained at length. "So I was more than a little disturbed to learn she wanted to live there, knowing my neglect may have been the impetus for her sentiments."

Elizabeth deemed it necessary to explain what her feelings had been in the wake of his absence. Finally, and at length, she confessed, "I thought you despised me for mishandling your letter."

"Despise you?" Mr. Darcy took Elizabeth in his arms. He could not have stopped himself from doing so, even if he tried.

"Oh, you of such little faith. Whatever am I to do with you? Do you know nothing about me at all?" He leaned closer and kissed Elizabeth softly on her forehead. He whispered in her ear, "When I fell in love with you, I fell in love with you forever."

Holding Elizabeth in his arms that way was something he had never done before—not like that. He held her as only a lover would. It felt right. The time had come for a second proposal, for he never wished to be parted from her ever again.

He kissed Elizabeth again, this time on her cheek and with such tenderness.

"Surely your feelings for me are not the same as they were last April. I have repeatedly avowed my love for you, and I have done everything in my power to prove myself worthy of you. Pray, say you love me. All the love I have in my heart is waiting for you. Say you will be mine."

"Yes!" Elizabeth said softly and without hesitation. "I love you, Mr. Darcy, with all my heart and soul."

He smiled. "You cannot know how much I have longed to hear those words!" He hugged Elizabeth close. "However, at such a time as this, my happiness is best conveyed with actions, not words." He kissed her on the corner of her mouth. He loved the taste of her lips. Oh, how he wished to kiss her properly. "You do trust me?"

Experiencing all the sensations of the moment, Elizabeth nodded.

Darcy took a few steps back, gathered Elizabeth by the hand, and began leading her to a more secluded spot—one in which they might remain in privacy for hours to come. Soon enough, he was kissing her in a way he had never done before.

Elizabeth lifted up her arms to give him better access to her body. Mr. Darcy's hands moved lower and lower to cup her derrière. He pulled their bodies closer together. Elizabeth knew and understood he was in her power, and she was in his as he continued to kiss her. The magnitude of his love was made apparent by the depth of his kisses, the lingering touch of his hands, and their bodies pressed close against each other. And they went on in that manner for a while.

Darcy's kisses became more and more ardent. Finally, he stopped to catch his breath as he rested his forehead against Elizabeth's, trying to control his ardor. This reprieve did not last very long—how were two lovers who ached for each other as they did to do otherwise? They could not get enough of each other.

Not all that transpired between Darcy and Elizabeth comprised making love—some conversation must be enjoyed and eventually a light repast. Having anticipated their needs when they met at their particular place so many times in the past, doing so that morning was second nature to Elizabeth. The basket she had brought along was filled with a fragrant mixture of apples, pears, oranges, strawberries, and grapes, cold ham slices, cheese, and baked bread. Darcy and Elizabeth found themselves too hungry to ignore the food she brought along. They shared their meal, at times feeding each other, finished with passionate kisses, and then got up for a walk.

They walked on without knowing in what direction. There was too much to be thought, and felt, and said for attention to any other objects. At length, the sun high above the sky reminded them that Elizabeth had stayed away too long. Surely her family would wonder where she was by now. It was time to return to Longbourn, only they returned together, hand in hand—intent on sharing their joyful news.

It was a whirlwind of excitement for the lovers in the weeks that followed. Elizabeth returned her betrothed's feelings in the most satisfying ways. Their passions never ceased to reign, which meant their whereabouts regularly went unaccounted for.

Elizabeth could not wait to become Mrs. Darcy. Part of her had wished for the appellation longer than even she knew. She told Jane as much when the two of them talked about all the joys that awaited them in matrimony. No one could have been happier for her than her dearest sister, Jane. As for her dear friend Mitchell, he would not say he was unhappy for Elizabeth. Instead, he declared her happiness was his happiness. If Mr. Darcy was the man to satisfy her every wish for future felicity in marriage, who was he to complain?

For Mr. Darcy's part, his passions for Elizabeth flowed more freely during the long, empty nights when they were forced to be apart. Alone in his bed at night, his desire for her knew no bounds, for within the confines of his dreams, he knew her as a man knew the only woman he had ever loved and would love for the rest of his life. Mornings would find him with one consistent thought on his mind—their wedding night. Then he would truly make her his wife.

CHAPTER 23

THE HAPPIEST WOMAN

With the marriage of three daughters in under three months, Mrs. Bennet's primary employment in life was almost done. For that, she could not have been more delighted. But of the two happier occasions among the three, Elizabeth's marriage to Mr. Darcy surprised her the most.

Not that the lady was disappointed by her family's good fortunes. Mrs. Bennet really did not know what to think. "I thought Lizzy was halfway in love with Mr. Hemmingsworth," she sometimes opined to her daughter Mary.

"I think we all did," was generally Mary's reply.

Of course, one could not always be correct, but to be mistaken with such magnitude—how could that be?

Mrs. Bennet was sure of one thing; Jane's marriage was nothing compared to Elizabeth's.

Mr. Bennet's self-imposed censure made him a far less negligent father. Never would one of his daughters suffer his inattention or his ridicule again. Elizabeth's removal to Derbyshire left ample empty space in his home and in his heart—the kind that could only be filled by a most beloved child. He missed her dearly, which indeed explained his frequent and unexpected arrivals at Pemberley.

As for Wickham and Lydia, their characters suffered no revolution from the marriages of the older sisters. They were always living beyond their means and relying on the generosity of both Elizabeth and Jane to make up all their deficits. And though Darcy could never receive the husband at Pemberley, he assisted him further in his profession, for Elizabeth's sake.

Elizabeth would always love her intimate friend, Charlotte, and her feelings toward the husband were about the same as they ever were. Mr. Collins was ridiculous. And though there was no mention of a future visit to Pemberley in any of the friends' letters, surely the Darcys and the Collinses knew the reason why.

It should have been me. One might well imagine

those five words at the heart of Mr. Bingley's regular refrain. Indeed, they were for a while. Time and distance, however, had a way of erasing the pangs of a broken heart. It would be some time still before he felt up to the task of falling in love again. When he did, nothing anyone could say—not even his best friend, Mr. Darcy—would persuade him otherwise.

Bingley's sisters did not return with him to Netherfield as he had planned. Indeed, he gave up the place entirely. Jane's marriage to Stanford Hemmingsworth had spared a familial connection to the pernicious sisters, which could not be a bad thing. However, as they were Bingley's relations and Bingley was Darcy's friend, their right of visiting Pemberley was thus retained.

Pemberley was now Georgiana's home, just as Darcy had hoped it would be once he and Elizabeth were married. The attachment of the sisters was exactly what it ought to have been. Georgiana's affection for her cousin Anne remained intact. When Georgiana was not in Derbyshire, she would often be in Kent, and likewise for Anne.

Lady Catherine had overplayed her hand when threatening to strip Darcy of his legal rights as Georgiana's co-guardian. He likened her ladyship's extortion to his former friend George Wickham's many schemes, which was really saying something. Despite the familial ties, he determined to have nothing more to do with his aunt. However, at Georgiana's insistence, he was willing to let bygones be bygones. In that vein, Darcy wrote to his aunt to tell her of his engagement to Elizabeth.

Lady Catherine never conceded to the idea of Darcy not marrying Anne. On the contrary, she was highly indignant at the thought of his marrying someone so far below the Fitzwilliam family's station in life. She gave way to all the genuine frankness of her character in her reply to the letter that announced its arrangement. She sent him language so very abusive, especially of Elizabeth, that all intercourse was at an end for a long time.

Mitchell was more than merely a second son; Mrs. Hemmingsworth had argued upon learning of his commission. Stanford was his father's heir, but being the spare heir was not nothing. She wanted both her sons nearby. If that made her selfish, then so be it. Yes, she had gained a beautiful daughter who ideally suited her elder son in every way and was an excellent mistress of Grandover Park, but was it fair that she might risk the loss of her other son? It was Stanford's argument to his mother to let a man be a man that won the day.

Elizabeth now had two brothers—but Wickham hardly counted in her mind. Between her only deserving brother-in-law and his twin brother, she really loved Mitchell more, even though Stanford had made Jane the happiest woman in all of England.

Or rather the second happiest, for Elizabeth knew in her heart that she bore the distinction of being the happiest—the happiest, the most adored, and the most cherished. Mr. Darcy's daily affirmations of his love for her, as much as she relished hearing them, need not have been spoken in words. For day after day he proved himself just what a man violently in love with his wife ought to be.

The End

ALSO BY P. O. DIXON

Standalone

Somebody Else's Gentleman

Something to Think Of

Wait for Love

Most Ardently, Most Unknowingly in Love

A Favorite Daughter

Gravity

Expecting His Wife

The Means of Uniting Them

Designed for Each Other

Together in Perfect Felicity

Which that Season Brings

Christmas Sealed with a Kiss

Christmas, Love and Mr. Darcy

A Night with Mr. Darcy to Remember

By Reason, by Reflection, by Everything

Impertinent Strangers

Bewitched, Body and Soul

To Refuse Such a Man

Miss Elizabeth Bennet

Still a Young Man

Love Will Grow

Only a Heartbeat Away

As Good as a Lord

Matter of Trust

Expecting His Proposal

Pride and Sensuality

A Tender Moment

Almost Persuaded

Series

Everything Will Change

Lady Elizabeth

So Far Away

Dearest, Loveliest Elizabeth

Dearest Elizabeth

Loveliest Elizabeth

Dearest, Loveliest Elizabeth

A Darcy and Elizabeth Love Affair

A Lasting Love Affair

'Tis the Season for Matchmaking

Pride and Prejudice Untold

To Have His Cake (and Eat it Too)

What He Would Not Do

Lady Harriette

Darcy and the Young Knight's Quest

He Taught Me to Hope

The Mission

Hope and Sensibility

Visit http://podixon.com for more.

ABOUT THE AUTHOR

P. O. Dixon is a writer as well as an entertainer. Historical England and its days of yore fascinate her. She, in particular, loves the Regency period with its strict mores and oh so proper decorum. Her ardent appreciation of Jane Austen's timeless works set her on the writer's journey—swapping boardrooms for ballrooms and never looking back.

CONNECT WITH THE AUTHOR

Twitter: @podixon
Facebook: facebook.com/podixon
Website: podixon.com
Newsletter: bit.ly/SuchHappyNews
Email: podixon@podixon.com

Manufactured by Amazon.ca
Bolton, ON